# A HEARTBEAT AWAY

Report of the
Twentieth Century Fund Task Force
on the Vice Presidency

Background Paper by
Michael Nelson

# A Heartbeat Away

**PP** Priority Press Publications/New York/1988

The Twentieth Century Fund is a research foundation undertaking timely analyses of economic, political, and social issues. Not-for-profit and non-partisan, the Fund was founded in 1919 and endowed by Edward A. Filene.

**Library of Congress Cataloging-in-Publication Data**
Nelson, Michael
  A heartbeat away

  Includes bibliographies and index.
  1. Vice-Presidents—United States. I. Twentieth Century
Fund. Task Force on the Vice Presidency.
II. Title
JK609.5.N45  1988        353.03'18        88-17942

ISBN 0-87078-230-4
ISBN 0-87078-229-0 (pbk.)

# Foreword

**D**uring discussions of the 1988 presidential election campaign, speculation has focused not only on the best candidate, that is, the candidate most likely to win the White House, but on the best "ticket." The public, the media, and politicians, in the course of these discussions, have considered, as possible partners on a winning ticket, some of the most able and experienced national political figures. Clearly, the vice presidency has become an office to be filled by someone Americans would consider a valid candidate for the presidency itself.

The vice president, moreover, has become more than the president's understudy. Once derided, the vice presidency now comes with a budget and staff, office space, and a number of executive functions. These changes raise a number of questions both about the way in which the vice president is chosen and the nature of the office held by the vice president.

The Trustees and staff of the Fund, long interested in the way Americans go about choosing their presidents, believed that attention also should be focused on the choice of the presidential running mate—and the responsibilities of the vice presidency. As a result, the Fund set up an independent Task Force comprised of politicians, scholars, journalists, and experts on government to consider the rules governing succession as well as such questions as how the current vice presidential selection process could be improved, what responsibilities the vice president should be assigned, and even the merits of having such an office.

*v*

The members of the Task Force had many lively discussions that dealt with practically every aspect of the vice presidency. Under the able chairmanship of Jack Watson, they have produced a report, with some dissents, that should be useful in choosing candidates for the office. The Fund is grateful to them for their efforts. The Fund and the members of the Task Force are also grateful to Michael Nelson of Vanderbilt University for the background paper that informed their deliberations.

M. J. Rossant, DIRECTOR
The Twentieth Century Fund
May 1988

# Contents

**Foreword** by M. J. Rossant                                                    *v*

**Members of the Task Force**                                                    *ix*

**Report of the Task Force**                                                      1
Comments by Hugh Heclo, Henry F. Reuss, and
Arthur M. Schlesinger, Jr.                                                       17

**Background Paper** by Michael Nelson                                           19
  1. Introduction                                                      21
  2. Origins and Development                                           25
  3. Selection                                                         41
  4. Activities                                                        61
  5. Succession and Disability                                         79
  6. Recommendations                                                   95
  Notes                                                                103
  Index                                                                111

# Members of the Task Force

**Jack H. Watson, Jr.,** *chairman*
Partner, Long, Aldridge & Norman, Atlanta, Georgia

**James Cannon**
Coexecutive Director, American Agenda, Washington, D.C.

**Leonard Garment**
Partner, Dickstein, Shapiro & Morin, Washington, D.C.

**Hugh Heclo**
Clarence J. Robinson Professor of Public Affairs, George Mason University, Fairfax, Virginia

**Richard Moe**
Partner, Davis, Polk & Wardwell, Washington, D.C.

**Roger Mudd**
Special Correspondent, MacNeil/Lehrer Newshour

**George Reedy**
Nieman Professor of Journalism, Marquette University, Milwaukee, Wisconsin

**Henry F. Reuss**
Former Chairman, House Committee on Banking, Finance and Urban Affairs and Joint Economic Committee

**Catherine Rudder**
Executive Director, American Political Science Association, Washington, D.C.

**Arthur M. Schlesinger, Jr.**
Albert Schweitzer Professor in the Humanities, Graduate School and University Center of the City University of New York

**Michael Nelson,** *rapporteur*
Associate Professor of Political Science, Vanderbilt University, Nashville, Tennessee

# REPORT OF THE
# TASK FORCE

Recent American history has given new prominence to the office of the vice presidency. Created almost by accident, held in small esteem for more than a century, the office has only in the last generation been seen as one of critical importance. Today's voters and, especially, the media display intense interest in the presidential candidates' choices of running mates, partly because those choices reveal the presidential candidates' judgment and taste and partly because the vice presidency is insurance in case of a future tragedy. The sitting vice president, moreover, is far more visible than ever before, more subject to public and media scrutiny.

Historically, nine vice presidents—more than one-fifth of those who have held the office—have succeeded to the presidency upon the death or resignation of the incumbent president; four others have gone on to be elected president. Today, the vice president is a presumptive candidate for president, and also a presumptive front-runner for his party's nomination; five of the seven most recent vice presidents subsequently received their parties' nomination in their own right, and George Bush seems certain to make it six of eight. Four of the five vice presidents who have succeeded to the presidency in this century later were elected to that office. The exception, Gerald R. Ford, came very close, as did the two most recent incumbent vice presidents to be nominated for president, Richard M. Nixon and Hubert H. Humphrey. For all the attention to the much-ballyhooed "Van Buren effect" (that is, that since Martin Van Buren in 1836, vice presidents have not been elected directly from the vice presidency to the presidency), no other office in recent years brings its incumbent as close to the White House as the vice presidency.

The modern vice presidency has also become an important and visible political institution. The vice president's access to the president and to staff, budget, and other resources has grown substantially in recent years. So have the duties that presidents, now almost as a matter of course, assign their vice presidents, both as diplomatic and political envoys and as confidential senior advisers. The growth of the importance of the role was made clear by the Twenty-fifth Amendment (1967), which assigned the vice president critical new roles in situations of presidential disability and created a mechanism to assure that the office would never remain vacant for long.

Despite these changes in the importance of the vice presidency, most discussions of the office are mired in hoary stereotypes. Pundits invariably trot out the familiar old quotes about the office—"not worth a pitcher of warm spit" (John Nance Garner), "not a crime exactly . . . but it's kind iv a disgrace" (Mr. Dooley), the vice president's only job is "to ring the White House bell every morning and ask what is the state of health of the president" (Thomas Marshall), and so on. Proposals for reforming the vice presidency—other than abolition—usually fall into one of two categories. Some start from the belief that, since the president is overburdened and the vice president has little to do, the pressure on the president should be relieved by assigning some responsibilities to the vice president. Others start with the assumption that, because the vice presidency is merely the successor office to the presidency and its lack of powers and duties discourages worthy political leaders from aspiring to the office, the role of the vice president should be made more substantial and thus more appealing.

To be sure, the vice presidency is not perfect. Strong arguments can be made that the office should never have been created by the framers of the Constitution and that it now should be abolished. *But a majority of the Task Force believes that, practically speaking, two centuries of history have woven the vice presidency into the fabric of the American constitutional order. The majority also believes that in recent times it has become a more prominent and, on balance, a more promising and constructive office.*

The Task Force also strongly believes that understanding how and why the vice presidency has attained its present status is critical to ensuring that many familiar reform ideas, most of them unhelpful and outdated, are dropped from the political agenda, and that new ideas, designed to improve and enhance some recent aspects of the office, replace them. Specifically, *the members of the Task Force strongly reject recent suggestions that the vice president should be assigned an additional executive position, such as secretary of a department or head of an executive agency.*

## Abolish the Vice Presidency?

The vice presidency was a late, even casual, creation of the Constitutional Convention, designed mainly to buttress the electoral college method of choosing the president. Because the electoral college was created in an era of strong local attachments, the Constitution initially called on electors, when voting for the president, to "vote by ballot for two persons, of whom one at least shall not be an Inhabitant of the same State with themselves." To assure that both votes would be cast seriously, the office of vice president was established for the runner-up in the presidential election; its occupant was to assume the powers and duties of the president (but not the office itself) in the event of the president's removal, death, resignation, or disability. The historical record also indicates that the framers intended that the vice president's role as acting president would last only until a special presidential election could be held, but this was not stated clearly in the Constitution.

Two important developments during the nineteenth century undermined the framers' intentions with respect to the vice presidency. First, political parties quickly formed and began nominating candidates for both president and vice president. As a result, the original electoral college, unsuited for party competition, broke down: in 1800, Thomas Jefferson and his vice presidential running mate, Aaron Burr, received an equal number of votes for president. Although the Twelfth Amendment (1804), which prevented recurrences of this calamity by forcing electors to vote separately for president and vice president, removed the framers' original rationale for having a vice president, efforts to abolish the office itself failed. Instead, it devolved from its original status as the office awarded to the second-most successful presidential candidate to a political consolation prize for largely undistinguished party politicians.

Another nineteenth-century development was the resolution (initially by assertion, then by custom) of the constitutional ambiguities regarding the vice president's status when the presidency became vacant in favor of full vice presidential succession to the presidency for the duration of the departed president's term. Although presidential succession acts in force from 1792 to 1947 mandated a special presidential election if both the elected president and vice president left office before their original four-year terms had expired, in the absence of any surviving delegates to the Constitutional Convention or published records of its proceedings, Vice President John Tyler successfully claimed the presidency when President William Henry Harrison died in 1841. Later vice presidents followed his example.

In view of the early history of the vice presidency, the argument that the office never should have been created (or, at least, that it should have been abolished as part of the Twelfth Amendment) is strong. So is the presumption that a vacancy in the presidency should be filled by a special election. Indeed, some members of the Task Force regard these proposals as appealing even now.*

Although the Task Force considers the idea of special presidential elections serious and provocative (not least because it conforms to the constitutionally stated ideal that the president "be elected"), a majority rejects it for two main reasons. First, on a pragmatic note, two centuries of constitutional history have imbedded the vice presidency both in our national political institutions and in the public consciousness. Even with its inherent constraints and limitations, the vice presidency is part of our political heritage and tradition and should not be discarded unless there are powerful and compelling reasons to do so. The majority does not think that those reasons exist. Second, and the majority of the Task Force believes even more important, the vice presidency in recent years has begun to evolve into a more useful and valuable institution.

Simply stated, the overriding reason for having a vice president is to ensure that there is someone who is well prepared to assume the presidency on a moment's notice. The advantage of the vice presidency is that the person who holds the office, if the president permits it, can be as knowledgeable about the full range of government activities and presidential decisions as the president. Although the vice president, like the copilot of a jumbo jet, is not in command of the plane, the vice president is there to assist the president in the discharge of his duties, and he is ready to assume the controls whenever it becomes necessary to do so. Like a copilot, the vice president may never be called upon to "fly the plane," but it is comforting to know that he is there to do so if the need arises. In addition, the majority of the members of the Task Force believe that there have been some significant strides in the role of the vice presidency in recent years in the areas of selection, duties, and succession. *Thus, the majority of the members of the Task Force believe that the evolution of the office under recent presidents has been constructive, and that the utilization of the vice president by the president should be encouraged and continued.*

---

* See Comments by Hugh Heclo, Henry F. Reuss, and Arthur M. Schlesinger, Jr., on pages 17–18.

## Selection

Selecting a vice presidential candidate is one of the most important decisions that a political party and its presidential nominee must make. Its importance derives mainly from the constitutional provision that, in case of the death, resignation, disability, or removal of the president from office, the vice president shall become president.

The good news is that, in general, twentieth-century vice presidents have been better qualified to be president than those of the nineteenth century, and better qualified in the second half of the twentieth century than in the first half. One measure, albeit imperfect, of this improvement is that although none of the four nineteenth-century vice presidents who succeeded to the office upon the death of the president—John Tyler, Millard Fillmore, Andrew Johnson, and Chester A. Arthur—was even nominated by his party to run for the presidency, all five twentieth-century successor presidents (Theodore Roosevelt, Calvin Coolidge, Harry S. Truman, Lyndon B. Johnson, and Gerald R. Ford) have been—and all but Ford were then elected. Another measure is the latest round of historians' ratings of the presidents; according to historians surveyed by Professor Robert K. Murray in 1981, the successor presidents of the nineteenth century included one failure (Andrew Johnson), two below-average presidents (Tyler and Fillmore), and only one who was even average (Arthur). As a group, the twentieth-century successor presidents actually rate higher than the elected presidents—two near-great presidents (Theodore Roosevelt and Truman), one above average (Lyndon Johnson), one average (Ford), and one below average (Coolidge).

The record of improvement in recent years is even more compelling. Since 1948, about half the vice presidential candidates—for example, Henry Cabot Lodge, Lyndon Johnson, Walter F. Mondale, and George Bush—have had more years of experience in high government office than the presidential candidates with whom they were running. In addition, about half the vice presidential candidates—for example, Earl Warren, Estes Kefauver, Hubert Humphrey, Lyndon Johnson, Mondale, and Bush—already had sought or been prominently mentioned for the presidency in their own right at the time they were picked.

To be sure, vice presidential nominees have been and will continue to be selected by the heads of their tickets and their parties mainly to help win elections. Nominations for vice president are, first and foremost, political choices. Certain kinds of ticket balancing—notably by region (North-South, East-West), religion (Protestant-Catholic), and experience

(Washington–state government)—continue to be practiced, but others, balancing ideological opposites for example, rarely come into play. And to the extent that balancing the ticket helps to unite a political party, it furthers a commendable goal.

What has changed is the weight given to the vice president's capacity to succeed to the presidency. The choice of a nominee who seems less than competent or who differs substantially from the presidential candidate on the issues no longer passes unremarked. Instead, such a nomination invites a barrage of critical commentary by the press, negative advertising by the opposition, and embarrassment in network television debates between the vice presidential candidates. Ultimately, the price of a rash or overly "political" nomination for vice president is paid in the coin of the electoral realm: votes on election day.

The public's increased concern with the competency of the vice president can be explained in large part by the visibility of the office in an age of pervasive national government and electronic communications. Since World War II, moreover, the United States has assumed the role of leader of the Western alliance in a world beset by new technologies that make instant and total nuclear war a possibility. If, as Samuel Johnson said, the prospect of a hanging "concentrates [the] mind wonderfully," so has the possibility that the vice president will inherit the presidential office on short notice concentrated some share of the public mind on the selection of vice presidents.

Parties and presidential candidates in search of victory have responded to these new public concerns. Jimmy Carter, like most recent presidential candidates, was able to sew up his nomination well in advance of the convention. His advisers developed a list of potential running mates; prospective nominees were then asked to provide extensive information about their backgrounds and finances and invited for long discussions with Carter. The process resulted in the selection of a vice presidential nominee, Walter Mondale, with whom Carter worked well during the campaign and in office.

Ronald Reagan's selection of Bush in 1980, although based on a less thorough search, demonstrates the political importance presidential candidates now attach to meeting public concerns about the vice presidency. Reagan seriously considered as potential running mates only those who already had undergone intense public scrutiny while running for or serving as president, notably Bush and former president Ford.

As the incentives for presidential candidates and their parties to seek out talented political leaders for vice president have grown, so have the incentives for such leaders to accept a vice presidential nomination. (One new disincentive—intense preselection scrutiny—also has been created, but it is hardly unique to the vice presidency.) Far from being a political dead end, the vice presidency is now the main stepping-stone to a party's presidential nomination. Beginning with Nixon, every vice president who has sought his party's presidential nomination has succeeded. As noted earlier, no one since Van Buren has done what Bush hopes to do in 1988—that is, be elected president while serving as vice president—but several have come very close and nine have become president through succession.

Thus, there have been noteworthy recent improvements in the vice presidential selection process. Perhaps more important, these improvements are grounded in political realities that are likely to endure. Even now, the selection process does not assure that vice presidential nominees who are qualified to be president will always be chosen. But, we suspect, it would be as impossible to devise a foolproof system for the selection of vice presidential candidates as it is to devise one for selecting presidential nominees.

The speed with which vice presidential candidates are selected can still create serious problems. Even early winners of their parties' presidential nomination, like Carter, have only a limited time to make one of their most important decisions; candidates whose fight for the nomination lasts until the convention run the risk of having to pick a running mate in less than a day. Experienced politicians are well aware of the dangers involved in making such an important decision in the frenzied atmosphere of a candidate's hotel suite in the early hours of the morning.

The Task Force believes that this problem can be alleviated without the passage of a new law or a constitutional amendment. Instead, *the Task Force recommends that the press and the parties bring the issue of the choice of a vice president to the candidates' attention frequently during the primary campaign just as they would any other important presidential election issue.*

Moreover, *the Task Force recommends that the two national party chairs request that their parties' presidential candidates institute a process for the evaluation of potential running mates at the earliest feasible time.* The evaluation process that a candidate decides to employ— questionnaires, interviews, informal inquiries, polling, or a mix of these— is less important than the creation of the process itself.

The press should include questions about the procedures the candidate has established for evaluating potential vice presidents on the list of major questions it asks of the presidential candidates. Such an effort will be fruitless, of course, if platitudinous answers are allowed to pass unchallenged. The press also should bear in mind that the more frequently such questions are asked, the more likely candidates will be to think about answers and act on them.

## Duties

Historically, there has been much uncertainty as to what role the chief understudy could play beyond serving as a living reminder to presidents of their own mortality. The Constitution states clearly that the "executive Power" is indivisibly invested in the president, and until very recently, the vice presidency was not thought of as a primarily executive office. For example, when President Dwight D. Eisenhower delegated tasks to Vice President Nixon, he was always careful to define these assignments as "requests" because he believed that the vice presidency was a legislative office. Eisenhower's view has a strong constitutional foundation— the vice president's only ongoing role, described in Article I, is to preside over the Senate, casting tiebreaking votes. Although the real meaning of the vice presidency derives from its relationship to the executive branch, and practice increasingly has defined the vice presidency as mainly executive in character (Nixon reported that he spent 90 percent of his time on executive matters), questions about the executive functions that the vice president can and should undertake remain unresolved.

In addition to analyzing the effects of the vice presidency on the presidency, observers of the office have thought long and hard about its effects on the vice president. Is service in the office a "making" or a "maiming" experience? Clearly, the vice president's relationship to the president must be confidential and subordinate; to become vice president is to be bound, by tradition if not by law, to the president's public policies and private direction. This status forces vice presidents to mute the very qualities of independence and leadership that brought them to their position and that would, if the call should come, invigorate their presidencies. The evisceration of the vice president is hardly inevitable— the generally successful record of the century's successor presidents demonstrates that—but clearly it is more likely to occur if the duties of the office are not substantial and challenging.

Thus, to enhance the usefulness of the vice presidency, the Task Force has developed three general precepts for future presidents that derive from the simple premise that the most important duty of the vice president is to be ready at all times to succeed to the presidency and that the correlative duty of the president is to see that the vice president is prepared to do so.

• *The Task Force recommends that presidents should continue the practice established by their most recent predecessors, presidents Ford, Carter, and Reagan, of granting the vice president complete access to the classified and confidential material that is available to the president.* The extent, importance, and complexity of the U.S. role in world affairs do not leave room for an information gap between the president and the person who is constitutionally charged to be ready to assume the powers and duties of the presidency on sudden notice.

• *The Task Force believes that the president should reject the familiar suggestion that the way to enhance the vice presidency is to give the vice president a cabinet post or any specific managerial responsibility.* Historically, the two vice presidents who have been assigned such positions—Henry A. Wallace, who served as chairman of the Board of Economic Warfare, and Nelson A. Rockefeller, who served as head of the White House Domestic Council—abandoned their assignments in failure. An executive position may place the vice president in an uncomfortable and publicly adversarial relationship with both the president and other appointed officials. Moreover, unlike all other appointees, the vice president cannot be removed from the administration by the president. Such a position also focuses the vice president's attention on one policy area, however important that area may be, reducing the vice president's general preparedness for succession.

• *The Task Force also recommends that the president and Congress provide the vice president with the resources needed to prepare for succession to the presidency and to carry out other responsibilities that are assigned by the president.* Although for many years the resources of the vice presidency were woefully inadequate, recent vice presidents have been able to add to the resources of the office and preserve the gains of their predecessors, thereby adding substantially to the "institutionalization" of the vice presidency. Specifically, Johnson was given a suite of offices in the Old Executive Office Building (previous vice presidents had worked at the Capitol); Agnew gained a line item for the vice president's office in the executive budget; Ford upgraded the quality and pay of the vice president's staff;

Rockefeller obtained a weekly private lunch with the president (along with a vice presidential mansion and a new seal of office); and Mondale was given an office in the West Wing, the right to attend all presidential meetings, and full access to the flow of papers to and from the president. Bush, with the approval of President Reagan, was the full beneficiary of the successful efforts of his predecessors.

The Task Force, in general, applauds these improvements in the vice president's capacity to serve the president and to prepare for the presidency. Although the Task Force has not focused its attention specifically on the optimal size of the vice president's budget and staff, the current budget and staff of the vice president's office appear to be adequate.

*The Task Force also urges that each president and vice president define their working relationship, taking into account their temperaments, experiences, and strengths as well as their views of executive leadership.* When, as has been the case in recent administrations, presidents trust and respect their vice presidents, they may want to adopt the following suggestions:

• *Whenever possible, the vice president should serve as general adviser to the president on the full range of presidential issues and concerns.* Presidents may wish to rely on vice presidents in this way in order to give them experience in the broad array of policy areas that they need to be familiar with if they have to assume the presidency. After all, the vice president is first and foremost an understudy to the president, and an understudy cannot be of much use if he knows only a fraction of the star's lines. Recent presidents also have found that it can be in their interest to use the vice president as a wide-ranging senior adviser, especially because the vice president is among the most experienced politicians in the White House and one of the few members of the president's official family who is not burdened with specific assignments.

• *The Task Force also recommends that the president assign the vice president other responsibilities that do not conflict with the role of general adviser.* Among these is the occasional use of the vice president as a special presidential envoy in foreign affairs. Because the vice president enjoys a position of great esteem in other countries, messages communicated to foreign leaders or to their people by the vice president often carry more force than those sent through normal channels. The vice president can perform a similar diplomatic role domestically. Because other public officials and political leaders may be more willing to speak frankly to the vice president than to the president, the vice president also can be a useful sounding board for the administration and give the president a fuller sense of what Congress and the rest of the political community are thinking. And, of course, the vice president usually is the administration's most effective public and party advocate, speaking as proxy for the president.

## Succession

Every concern about the vice presidency is, in the end, a concern about succession. Selecting a vice presidential candidate can be instrumental in uniting a political party or winning the general election, but what makes vice presidential selection critically important is the possibility that the vice president may succeed to the presidency. Although lodging duties and investing resources in the vice presidency can make vice presidents useful agents and advisers of the administration, none of that is as important as preparing the vice president to become president. *The Task Force believes that the incentives are stronger than at any time in history to select capable political leaders to serve as vice president and to invest them with sufficient duties and resources to prepare them to be president.*

There are, in addition, issues meriting discussion relating to the process of succession itself, both permanent succession (which occurs after the president dies, resigns, or is removed) and temporary succession (when the president is disabled). Most of these issues arise from the Twenty-fifth Amendment.

Section 2 of the amendment provides that "whenever there is a vacancy in the office of the Vice President, the President shall nominate a Vice President who shall take office upon confirmation by a majority vote of both Houses of Congress." Although the purpose of this section is to insure that a vice president will always be in place to succeed to the presidency if needed, nothing binds either Congress or the president to act promptly when a vice presidential vacancy occurs. In 1974, for example, 139 days elapsed between Ford's succession to the presidency and Congress's confirmation of his nomination of Rockefeller to be vice president. One hundred twenty-eight of those days were spent on the confirmation process.

Here, as in the case of selection and duties, *the Task Force believes that admonition and encouragement rather than laws or constitutional amendments offer the best solution to the problem of delays in the succession process.* To be sure, time limits could be imposed upon the president (to submit a nomination) and Congress (to vote upon it). To do so, however, would require a constitutional amendment, a remedy far out of proportion to the problem. It also would tie the hands of the president and especially Congress should an unusually troublesome nomination arise. The proper remedy for political footdragging on a vice presidential nomination, if that should take place, is, and likely would be, public pressure through the press and other channels to act responsibly.

The majority of the Task Force believes that the high degree of legitimacy that was enjoyed by the Ford-Rockefeller administration is a testimony to the effectiveness of the current constitutional arrangement. The sort of unusual, potentially turbulent circumstances that produce such administrations cry out for procedures that, although equally unusual, are certain and stabilizing. Section 2 of the Twenty-fifth Amendment is in keeping with these criteria. It also preserves at least the spirit of normal vice presidential selection. For the president to nominate the vice president is a well-accepted practice of modern electoral politics; that both houses of Congress scrutinize and confirm the president's vice presidential nominee is a not unreasonable substitute for popular election. Finally, Section 2 enjoys considerable legitimacy simply by virtue of being a duly enacted constitutional procedure.

The Task Force also expressed some concern for problems related to the presidential disability provisions of the Twenty-fifth Amendment. Section 3 authorizes the president, when "unable to discharge the powers and duties of his office," to transfer those powers and duties temporarily to the vice president by writing a simple letter to the president pro tempore of the Senate and the speaker of the House of Representatives. A subsequent letter, sent by the president when once again able, ends the transfer.

*The Task Force believes that presidents should not be reluctant to transfer power to the vice president whenever they are incapacitated by anesthesia, serious illness, or injury.* The stigma of weakness or instability will be attached to such transfers only if they are made rarely and shamefacedly; if Section 3 is applied routinely, these stigma will disappear entirely. *The Task Force believes that presidents should announce, publicly and early in their administrations, the circumstances in which they will invoke Section 3 and the procedures they will use to decide whether those circumstances exist.* Failing such initiatives, public pressure to act responsibly will encourage presidents to understand that the politically wise course and the statesmanlike course are one.

A second difficulty regarding presidential disability, covered in Section 4 of the Twenty-fifth Amendment, involves situations in which the president may be disabled but is unable or unwilling to say so. In this case, the amendment provides that "the Vice President and a majority of either the principal officers of the executive departments or of such other body as Congress may by law provide" agree to transfer the powers and duties of the presidency to the vice president until either the president's disability passes or the four-year term expires. Some members of the Task Force thought that Congress should, in such cases, exercise its option under the amendment to pass a law to replace the heads of the departments, a diverse and perhaps unwieldy group, with a smaller body, perhaps the three senior department heads (the secretaries of state, treasury, and defense).

Despite this suggestion, *the majority of the Task Force regards the full complement of department heads as the best group to share responsibility with the vice president in determinations of presidential disability.* In keeping with Section 4, it believes that the group should be one that the president has appointed, to mute any possibility of charges of coups d'etat when power is taken from the president. It also agrees that, given the nation's diversity, the group should be diverse. As to size, a group of fourteen (the present size of the cabinet plus the soon-to-be-established secretary of veterans' affairs) is both large enough to resist conspiracy and small enough to assemble around one table and freely discuss the question at hand. Finally, the legislative history of Section 4 suggests that, although it entrusted Congress with the right to replace the cabinet in disability determinations, its principal intent was to deter a disabled but intransigent president from firing his department heads in order to prevent a determination of disability.

## Conclusion

The vice president's most important responsibility always has been to be prepared to be president at a moment's notice; in an era of superpower politics and nuclear armaments, this responsibility has become critical. When vice presidents are political leaders of demonstrated competence, when adequate information and resources are made available to them, and when succession procedures are followed with sensitivity and care, vice presidents are most likely to be adequately prepared. These conditions are most likely to be met when the parties, the press, presidential candidates, Congress, the president, and the vice president are aware of their duties and perform them responsibly. All of our recommendations are exhortations to that end.

# Comments

by
**Hugh Heclo**
**Henry F. Reuss, and**
**Arthur M. Schlesinger, Jr.**

We believe that long experience has proved the office of the vice president to be beyond redemption. The Constitution assigns no role to the vice president except to preside over the Senate, to cast a vote in case of a tie, and to succeed to the president's powers and duties in case of the death, disability, removal, or resignation of a president. Efforts have been made from time to time to invest the vice presidency with substance. These efforts have uniformly failed.

The only real point of the office is to provide for presidential succession. But far from preparing the occupant for the presidency, the frustrations inseparable from the office have made it as often a maiming as a making experience, a process of emasculation rather than of education.

The modern vice presidency that has developed with little forethought over the past thirty years is proving a more disruptive than constructive feature of our political system. First, the contemporary office both confers unfair political advantages on its holder in the contest for the presidential nomination and traps him, once nominated, into identification with policies that he may privately reject but could not, as vice president, publicly oppose—results that are bad for the incumbent party and bad for the country. Second, the recent development of a vice presidential bureaucracy with few real functions to perform and limited accountability to Congress increases the potential for mischief at the summit of government. Finally, the process of selecting vice presidential candidates in the heat of modern presidential campaigns has not worked reliably to produce qualified nominees; instead, the process has increasingly served to create a secondary personality contest in national elections. In short, there is a fundamental and growing contradiction between the *function* of providing for a worthy but temporary stand-in at the Oval Office and the *form* inherent in today's vice presidency.

For these reasons, we favor a return to the constitutional principle that a president "be elected" (Article II, Section 1) and to the principle enunciated by President Harry S. Truman in 1945 that no president should have the power to appoint his own successor. These two principles can be implemented in several ways to fill a vacancy in the presidency. One possibility would be a constitutional amendment abolishing the vice presidency and providing for a special election to be held ninety days after the death, disability, resignation, or removal of a president. In such cases, the acting president, who would serve until the president is elected, would be a member of the cabinet according to the order set forth in the Succession Act of 1886 (secretary of state, secretary of treasury, and so on). Should such a vacancy occur within 120 days of a regular biennial or quadrennial election, the acting president would serve until the next regular election.

# BACKGROUND PAPER

## by Michael Nelson

# Chapter 1
# Introduction

The vice presidency has long been an easy target of derisive humor, the running joke being that the office is of little consequence. Finley Peter Dunne, speaking through his invented character Mr. Dooley, described the vice presidency as "not a crime exactly. Ye can't be sint to jail f'r it, but it's kind iv a disgrace. It's like writin' anonymous letters." One motif of George S. Kaufman and Morrie Ryskind's popular 1930s musical, *Of Thee I Sing,* was the ongoing effort of Vice President Alexander Throttlebottom to find two references so that he could get a library card. Some vice presidents have joined in the fun. Thomas R. Marshall compared himself to "a man in a cataleptic fit; he cannot speak; he cannot move; he suffers no pain; he is perfectly conscious of all that goes on, but has no part of it." John Nance Garner derided his job as "not worth a pitcher of warm spit." (That's a G-rated version of what he said.) Even scholars have given way to merriment at the thought of the vice presidency "The chief embarrassment in discussing the office," wrote Professor Woodrow Wilson, "is, that in explaining how little there is to say about it one has evidently said all there is to say."[1] Clinton Rossiter spent 7 of 281 pages on the vice presidency in his book *The American Presidency,* then apologized that "even this ratio of forty to one is no measure of the vast gap between [the two offices] in power and prestige."[2]

Many a truth—about the vice presidency as well as other things—has been spoken in jest, of course. Constitutionally, the vice presidency was born weak and has not grown much stronger. But lost in all the laughter is an appreciation of the importance—ongoing in American history but

21

growing in recent years—of the position the vice presidency occupies in the American political system. The office is most significant, of course, when, cocoonlike, it empties itself to provide a successor to the presidency. ("I am vice president," said the first person to hold the office, John Adams. "In this I am nothing, but I may be everything.") Nine vice presidents, more than a fifth of those who have been selected for the office, have become president when the incumbent died or resigned. Each of the twentieth century's five vice-presidents-turned-successor-presidents—Theodore Roosevelt, Calvin Coolidge, Harry S. Truman, Lyndon B. Johnson, and Gerald R. Ford—subsequently was nominated by his party for a full term, and all but Ford were elected. (Collectively, they led the nation for almost twenty-nine years, roughly a third of the century to date.)

In 1965, Congress decided that it was so important to have a vice president standing by at all times that it passed the Twenty-fifth Amendment, establishing a procedure for filling vice presidential vacancies. The amendment, ratified by the states in 1967, also stated unequivocally the right of the vice president, in the event of the president's death, resignation, or impeachment, to serve as president for the balance of the four-year term; in addition, it created a mechanism by which the vice president could assume the powers and duties of the presidency whenever and for as long as the president was disabled.

Besides its long-standing role as contingent presidential successor, the vice presidency has become an important electoral springboard to the presidency. The modern vice president is not only a presumptive candidate for president, but the presumptive front-runner and nominee of the party as well. Fifteen of nineteen twentieth-century vice presidents have gone on to seek the presidency. In the history of the Gallup poll, which extends back to 1936, Garner and every vice president since Richard M. Nixon have led in a majority of surveys measuring the voters' preferences for their party's presidential nomination.[3] Six of the eight most recent vice presidents, including George Bush, later were nominated for president in their own right.

Finally, recent changes in the vice presidency have made the office itself increasingly substantial. The vice presidency has become "institutionalized" to some degree.[4] This is true both in the narrow sense that it is organizationally larger and more complex than in the past (the vice president's staff, for example, has grown from twenty in 1960 to around seventy today) and in the broader sense that certain kinds of vice presidential activities now are taken for granted. These include: regular private meetings with the president, membership on the National Security Council, national security briefings, frequent diplomatic missions, public advocacy of the president's leadership and programs, party leadership, and others. Modern vice presidents have a lot more to do than, in Marshall's gibe, "ring the White House bell every morning and ask what is the state of health of the president."

The vice presidency, then, as successor, springboard, and institution, has become an important office. It also is a problematic one. Some of its problems are relatively new, others are long-standing, still others are long-standing but seem new because recent changes in the office have brought them into sharp relief. Among the problems of the vice presidency are these:

- Vice presidential candidates sometimes have been chosen by the two major parties in haste and with victory in the election, not governing afterward, uppermost in mind. Critics argue that the traditional nominating process is poorly designed to produce vice presidents of talent and ability. Others identify problems in the Twenty-fifth Amendment's procedure for vice presidential selection when a vacancy occurs in the office, which entails presidential nomination and congressional confirmation. They suggest, for example, that presidents typically will make bland selections in order to avoid a lengthy and perhaps losing fight in Congress.

- For all the newfound influence of the office, vice presidential power still is largely a function of the president's willingness to confer it. Vice presidents who wish to make the most of the position, therefore, are encouraged to keep their views anonymous, their behavior loyal, their attitude toward sometimes unpleasant presidential assignments dutiful, and their deportment self-effacing. (Those who deviate even slightly from this code may be regarded as untrustworthy by the president and, especially, by the White House staff.) All this has led Arthur M. Schlesinger, Jr., to suggest that the vice presidency is "much less a making than a maiming experience."[5]

- The ambiguous constitutional status of the vice presidency is the source of some concern. A variety of opinions and practices have emerged through the years. Vice President Thomas Jefferson, dwelling on the vice president's role as president of the Senate, said, "I consider my office as constitutionally confined to legislative duties." Garner placed the vice presidency in "a no man's land somewhere between the executive and legislative branch"; Walter F. Mondale said that as vice president he was "a member of both . . . branches." In practice, recent vice presidents (including Mondale) have served as adjuncts to the presidency, slighting their legislative responsibilities. Yet presidents are understandably reluctant to assign certain important tasks to vice presidents, knowing that, unlike department heads and other executive officials, they cannot be commanded, removed, or otherwise held formally accountable for their words and actions.[6]

• Numerous problems have been perceived in the succession arrangements that place the vice president first in line to be president in the event of a presidential vacancy or disability. For example, if vice presidents are selected in haste for short-term electoral reasons, then put to work in sometimes degrading ways, are they likely to be worthy successors to the presidency? Does vice presidential succession undermine the Constitution's larger concern that the president "be elected"? Does the Twenty-fifth Amendment, which allows for an endless string of appointed vice presidents succeeding to the presidency, fly in the face of democratic norms?

In sum, although the vice presidency is an increasingly important office, it is not devoid of problems.

# Chapter 2
# Origins and Development

The vice presidency has evolved through four fairly distinct eras: the founding period, which extended from the Constitutional Convention of 1787 until the enactment of the Twelfth Amendment in 1804; the nineteenth century, which was the office's nadir; the first half of the twentieth century, a period that began with the vice presidency of Theodore Roosevelt, was marked by greater vice presidential visibility but still minor functions, and ended with Harry S. Truman's sudden and dangerously unprepared succession to the presidency in 1945; and the modern era, in which the role of the vice president has been greater and perhaps has been institutionalized as well. During the first two eras, the remark of the first vice president, John Adams—"I am possessed of two powers; the one is *esse* [actual] and the other is *posse* [potential]"—was true because it was ironic. In the more recent periods, it has become true almost at face value.[1]

## The Founding Period

### Constitutional Origins

The Constitution contains the vice presidency's genetic code, its hereditary legacy from the act of conception. To be sure, both historical changes in the political environment of the office and the actions of individual presidents and vice presidents have substantially affected the development of the vice presidency. But the general contours within which the office's functions and influence have evolved have been shaped by the Constitution.

All the more surprising, then, that the invention of the vice presidency was an afterthought of the Constitutional Convention, a residue of its solution to the problem of presidential selection. Initially, the framers had agreed that the legislature should choose the executive, who, to remove the temptation to use the powers and patronage of the office to trade favors for votes with legislators in a quest for reelection, was to be allowed only one term. But as the convention wore on, delegates became so enamored of the incentive to excellent service in office provided by eligibility for reelection that they removed the restriction and, with it, the legislative method of presidential selection.[2]

How, then, to elect the president? Late in its proceedings, after rejecting a number of proposals, the convention turned the matter over to the Committee of Eleven (sometimes aptly referred to as the Committee on Postponed Matters). The committee's solution was the electoral college, a system by which each state chose electors who in turn chose the president by majority vote. A possibly fatal defect of this procedure—that state electors simply would vote for a variety of favorite sons, preventing the choice of a nationally elected president—was remedied by assigning the electors two votes each for president, requiring that they cast at least one of their votes for a candidate who "shall not be an Inhabitant of the same State with themselves," and—to assure that their second votes would not be used frivolously—attaching a consequence to them: the runner-up in the election for president would be awarded the newly created office of vice president.

Thus, as Hugh Williamson, a delegate to the convention from North Carolina and a member of the Committee of Eleven, testified, "Such an office as vice-President was not wanted. It was introduced only for the sake of a valuable mode of election which required two to be chosen at the same time."[3] But, having invented the vice presidency, the committee proposed that the office also be used to solve two other problems that had vexed the convention. The first was the role of president of the Senate. Some delegates had fretted that if a senator were chosen for this position (which customarily carried no vote on legislation except to break ties), the senator's state would be effectively denied half its representation. The committee recommended that, as a way around this problem, the vice president be president of the Senate.[4] Although a few delegates expressed concern that giving this role to the vice president would violate the principle of separation of powers, the convention assented.

The second loose end that the committee used the vice presidency to tie off involved presidential succession. The convention earlier had stipulated that the Senate president would assume the powers and duties of the presidency in the event of a vacancy. But that decision had displeased some delegates, who feared it would give the Senate a stake in presidential vacancies and suggested instead that the chief justice or a council of state fill the office. The committee then proposed that the vice president, who as runner-up in the presidential election could reasonably be judged the second-most qualified person in the country to be president, be designated as successor to the presidency. As will be described later, both the committee and the convention that accepted its recommendation almost certainly intended that the vice president would be acting president, assuming the powers and duties of the presidency but not the office itself, and would serve only until a special election could be held to choose a new president. But the Committee of Style, which was created to turn the convention's many decisions into a final draft of the Constitution, unwittingly blurred these intentions.

In all, the invention of the vice presidency was an ingenious solution to a number of problems related to the presidency and the Senate. As an office, however, it was inherently plagued by problems of its own. Its hybrid status was bound to make it suspect in legislative councils because it was partly executive and in executive councils because it was partly legislative. The single assigned responsibility of the vice presidency, to preside over the Senate, was almost trivial, yet were there not this duty, observed Roger Sherman of Connecticut, the vice president "would be without employment." The successor role was to be an inevitable source of tension between president and vice president, as well as of confusion. (The fabled "one heartbeat away" that separates the vice president from the presidency is, after all, the president's.) Finally, more than any other institution of the new government, the vice presidency required the realization of the framers' hopes that political parties would not emerge in the new nation. The office would seem less a brilliant than a rash improvisation of the convention if it were occupied as a matter of course by the president's leading partisan foe.[5]

## The Early Vice Presidency

Midway through his tenure as the nation's first vice president, John Adams lamented to his wife, Abigail, "My country has in its wisdom contrived for me the most insignificant office that ever the invention of man contrived or his imagination conceived." Little did Adams realize that the vice presidency was at a peak of influence during the period in which he served. Because the Senate was small and still relatively unorganized, Adams was able not only to cast twenty-nine tiebreaking votes (still the record), but to guide the upper house's agenda and intervene in debate. Adams also was respected and sometimes consulted on diplomatic and other matters by President George Washington, who invited him to meet with the cabinet in his absence. And, having won his office by receiving the second largest number of electoral votes for president in 1789 and 1792, it seemed only fitting that Adams should be chosen as Washington's successor.

Adams's election as president was different from Washington's, however. The framers' hopes notwithstanding, political parties emerged during the Washington administration. The result in 1796 was the election as vice president of the losing party's presidential nominee, Thomas Jefferson. Even before the inauguration, Adams tried to lure Jefferson into the administration's fold by urging him to undertake a diplomatic mission to France, but Jefferson, eager to build up his own party and win the presidency away from Adams, would have none of it. He justified his refusal by claiming that, constitutionally, the vice presidency was a legislative position.

Unsatisfied with the divided partisan result of the 1796 election, each party nominated a complete ticket in 1800, instructing its electors to cast their two votes for president for its presidential and vice presidential candidates. The intention was that both would be elected; the result was that neither was. The electors having voted as instructed, Jefferson and his vice presidential running mate, Aaron Burr, ended up with an equal number of votes for president. This outcome was doubly vexing: not only was Jefferson the party's clear choice for president, but there was little love lost between him and Burr, who had been placed on the ticket to balance the Virginia and New York wings of the party. Under the Constitution, the House of Representatives was called upon to choose between them. It eventually did, picking Jefferson, but not before opposition-party mischief-makers kept the result uncertain through thirty-six ballots. Burr was elected vice president.

One result of the election of 1800 was the Burr vice presidency, which was marked by bad relations between him and Jefferson and by several notorious incidents, including a duel in which Burr shot and killed Alexander Hamilton. Another was the widespread realization that something had to be done to reform the electoral college so that it could accommodate the existence of party competition. Vice presidential selection was the problem; one obvious solution was to force electors to vote separately for president and vice president. In opposing this suggestion, which was proposed as the Twelfth Amendment to the Constitution, some members of Congress argued that it would create a worse problem than it solved. Because "the vice president will not stand on such high ground in the method proposed as he does in the present mode of a double ballot" for president, predicted Samuel Taggert, the nation could expect that "great care will not be taken in the selection of a character to fill that office." William Plumer warned that such care as was taken would be "to procure votes for the president."[6] In truth, as the nomination of Burr indicated, the parties already had begun to degrade the vice presidency into a device for ticket balancing. Motions were made in Congress to abolish the office, rather than continue it in a form diminished from its original constitutional status as the position awarded to the second-most qualified person to be president, but they failed by votes of 12-19 in the Senate and 27-85 in the House. Instead, the Twelfth Amendment passed and entered the Constitution in 1804.[7]

## The Vice Presidency in the Nineteenth Century

The development of political parties and the enactment of the Twelfth Amendment sent an already constitutionally weak vice presidency into a tailspin that lasted until the end of the nineteenth century. Party leaders, not presidential candidates (who often were not even present at national conventions and, if present, were expected to be seen and not heard), chose the nominees for vice president, which certainly did not foster trust or respect between the president and vice president. Aggravating the tension were the main criteria that party leaders applied to vice presidential selection, namely, to placate the region or faction of the party that had been most dissatisfied with the presidential nomination, to win a state in the general election where the presidential candidate was not popular, or both. A certain measure of comity existed between a few nineteenth-century presidents and vice presidents—notably Andrew Jackson and Martin Van Buren, James K. Polk and George M. Dallas, Abraham Lincoln and Hannibal Hamlin, Rutherford B. Hayes and William A. Wheeler, and William McKinley and Garret A. Hobart, but even in these administrations, the vice president was not invited to cabinet meetings or entrusted with important tasks.

In addition to fostering tension within the government, ticket balancing as the main basis for vice presidential selection also placed such a stigma on the office that many politicians were unwilling to accept a nomination. (Daniel Webster, declining the vice presidential place on the Whig party ticket in 1848, said, "I do not propose to be buried until I am dead.")[8] Those who did accept and were elected found that fresh political problems four years after their nomination invariably led party leaders to balance the ticket differently; no first-term vice president ever was renominated for a second term by a party convention. Even the office's role as president of the Senate (which most vice presidents, following Jefferson's lead and for want of anything else to do, spent considerable time performing) became ever more ceremonial as the Senate institutionalized and took greater charge of its own affairs. John C. Calhoun was the last vice president whom the Senate allowed to appoint the members of its committees.

Not surprisingly, then, the nineteenth-century vice presidents make up a virtual rogues' gallery of personal and political failures. Because the office was so unappealing, an unusual number of the politicians who could be enticed to run for vice president were old and in bad health. Six died in office, all of natural causes: George Clinton, Elbridge Gerry, William R. King (who took his oath of office in Cuba and died the next month), Henry Wilson, Thomas A. Hendricks, and Hobart. Some vice presidents became embroiled in financial scandals: Daniel D. Tompkins was charged with keeping inadequate financial records while serving as governor of New York during the War of 1812, and Schuyler Colfax and Wilson were implicated in the Credit Mobilier scandal. Other vice presidents fell prey to personal scandals. Tompkins and Andrew Johnson were heavy drinkers (Johnson's first address to the Senate was a drunken harangue). Richard M. Johnson kept a series of slave mistresses, educating the children of one but selling another when she lost interest in him. Clinton, Calhoun, and Chester A. Arthur each publicly expressed his dislike for the president. Clinton refused to attend President James Madison's inauguration and openly attacked the administration's foreign and domestic policies. Calhoun alienated two presidents, John Quincy Adams and Jackson, by using his role as Senate president to subvert their policies and appointments, then resigned in 1831 to accept South Carolina's election as senator. Arthur attacked President James A. Garfield over a patronage quarrel. "Garfield has not been square, nor honorable, nor truthful . . .," he told the *New York World*. "It's a hard thing to say of a president of the United States, but it's only the truth."[9] Finally, some vice presidents did not even live in Washington—Richard Johnson left to run a tavern for a year.

Nonetheless, in one area of vice presidential responsibility—presidential succession—the nineteenth century witnessed a giant step forward. The succession question did not even arise until 1841, when William Henry Harrison became the first president to die in office. As noted earlier, the language of the Constitution provided little guidance about whether the vice president, John Tyler, was to become president for the remainder of Harrison's term or merely acting president until a special election could be held; the records of the Constitutional Convention, which could have clarified the framers' intentions, had long been kept secret and still were not widely available. In this uncertain situation, Tyler's claim to both the office and the balance of Harrison's term was accepted with little debate, setting a precedent that the next successor president, Millard Fillmore, was able to follow without any controversy at all.

Even this bright spot in the early history of the vice presidency was tarnished. Tyler's administration was marred by debilitating disagreements with the party, especially in Congress, and with the late president's cabinet. Fillmore and the other two nineteenth-century successor presidents, Andrew Johnson and Chester Arthur, encountered similar problems. None is regarded as having been a successful president—in the most recent and extensive round of historians' rankings, Johnson was rated a failure, Tyler and Fillmore as below average, and Arthur as average.[10] Nor were any of them nominated for a full term as president in their own right, much less elected. Finally, the issue of vice presidential responsibility during periods of presidential disability remained unresolved. During the seventy-nine days that President Garfield lay comatose before dying from an assassin's bullet in 1881, for example, Vice President Arthur could only stand by helplessly, lest he be branded a usurper.

## Theodore Roosevelt to Harry Truman

The rise of national news media (specifically mass-circulation magazines and newspaper wire services), a new style of active presidential campaigning, and some alterations in the vice presidential nominating process moderately enhanced the status of the vice presidency during the first half of the twentieth century. In 1900, the Republican nominee for vice president, Theodore Roosevelt, became the first vice presidential candidate (and, other than William Jennings Bryan, the first member of a national party ticket) to campaign vigorously around the country. While McKinley waged a sedate "front-porch" campaign for reelection, Roosevelt gave 673 speeches to three million listeners in twenty-four states.

The national reputation Roosevelt established through travel and the media stood him in good stead when he succeeded to the presidency after McKinley's assassination in 1901. Roosevelt was able to reverse the earlier pattern of successor presidents and set a new one: he was nominated by his party for a full term as president in 1904, as were Calvin Coolidge in 1924, Harry S. Truman in 1948, Lyndon B. Johnson in 1964, and Gerald R. Ford in 1976. Roosevelt's success also may help to explain another new pattern that contrasts sharply with nineteenth-century practice. Starting with James S. Sherman in 1912, every first-term vice president in the twentieth century who sought a second term has been nominated for reelection. Finally, Roosevelt helped lay the intellectual groundwork for an enhanced role for the vice president in office. In an 1896 article, he argued that the president and vice president should share the same "views and principles" and that the vice president "should always be . . . consulted by the president on every great party question. It would be very well if he were given a seat in the Cabinet . . . a [Senate] vote on ordinary occasions, and perchance a voice in the debates."[11]

Roosevelt was unable to practice what he preached about the vice presidency. Just as party leaders had forced Roosevelt's nomination for vice president on President McKinley to balance the old guard and progressive wings of the party in 1900, so did they impose the nomination of old guardsman Charles W. Fairbanks on him in 1904. But the enhanced political status of the vice presidency soon began to make it a more attractive office to at least some able and experienced political leaders, such as Charles Dawes, who had held office in three administrations and won a Nobel Prize; Charles Curtis, the Senate majority leader; and John Nance Garner, the speaker of the House. And, with somewhat more talent to offer, some vice presidents were given more responsibilities by the presidents they served. John Adams was the only vice president to meet with the cabinet prior to the twentieth century, for example, but when Woodrow Wilson went to Europe to negotiate the Versailles treaty (the first time a president had ever left U.S. soil), he asked Vice President Thomas R. Marshall to preside in his absence. Warren G. Harding invited Coolidge to meet with the cabinet as a matter of course, as has every president since Franklin D. Roosevelt.[12]

The Roosevelt years were marked by several innovations in the vice presidency. Franklin Roosevelt, like his cousin Theodore, had both run for vice president before becoming president (he lost in 1920) and written an article urging that the responsibilities of the vice presidency be expanded. In the article, Roosevelt identified four roles that the vice president could helpfully perform: cabinet member, presidential adviser, liaison to Congress, and policymaker in areas "that do not belong in the province" of any existing department or agency.[13] As president, he initially had so much respect for his vice president, former House speaker Garner, that even though the conservative Texan's nomination had been imposed on Roosevelt at the 1932 Democratic convention, he relied on Garner during the first term as "a combination presiding officer, cabinet officer, personal counselor, legislative tactician, Cassandra, and sounding board."[14] Most significantly, the vice president served as an important liaison from the president to Congress—it was Garner's suggestion that led to the practice, which subsequent presidents have followed, of meeting weekly with congressional leaders, with the vice president usually in attendance. Garner also undertook a goodwill mission abroad at Roosevelt's behest, another innovation that virtually all later administrations have continued. Early in his third term, Roosevelt appointed his new vice president, Henry A. Wallace (the president and Garner had had a falling out during the second term), to head the Economic Defense Board, an important agency for wartime preparation that was renamed the Board of Economic Warfare and assigned major procurement responsibilities after war was declared. (Wallace's tenure was highly controversial.) As the vice president's executive responsibilities increased, the legislative role diminished—Garner was the last vice president to fulfill the office of Senate president diligently.

Finally, two modifications of the party nominating conventions fostered greater harmony between presidents and vice presidents. In 1936, at Roosevelt's insistence, the Democrats abolished their two-thirds rule for presidential nominations, which meant that candidates for president no longer had to tolerate as much trading of vice presidential nominations and other administration posts to win at the convention. (They also abolished the two-thirds rule for vice presidential nominations, reducing the degree of consensus needed for that choice as well.) Four years later, Roosevelt completed his coup by seizing the party leaders' traditional prerogative to determine nominations for vice president. His tactic was simple: he threatened that, unless the convention chose Wallace (which it was loath to do), he would not accept its nomination for a third term.

Advances in the visibility, stature, and extraconstitutional responsibilities of the vice presidency may help to explain the office's improved performance as successor to the presidency, its main constitutional role. Historians rate two of the five twentieth-century successor presidents as near great (Theodore Roosevelt and Truman), one as above average (Johnson), one as average (Ford), and only one (Coolidge) as below average.[15] But for all its gains, at mid-century the vice presidency was still a fundamentally weak office. Its constitutional status was substantially unaltered, although the Twentieth Amendment (1933) did establish the full successorship of the vice-president-elect in the event of a president-elect's death. Ticket balancing to increase the party's appeal on election day continued to dominate vice presidential selection. All the ambiguities of the vice president's rights and duties in times of presidential disability still were unresolved, as dramatized by the ignorant-bystander role Marshall and Truman were forced to play during the severe illnesses of the two wartime presidents, Wilson and Franklin Roosevelt. Tension continued to mark some presidential pairings, at least until Roosevelt won presidential candidates the right to choose their running mates. (Theodore Roosevelt and Fairbanks, William Howard Taft and Sherman, Coolidge and Dawes, Herbert Hoover and Curtis, and Franklin Roosevelt and Garner during their second term did not get along well.) Even the glimmerings of enhanced vice presidential influence sometimes seemed to be no more than that: when Truman succeeded to the presidency upon Roosevelt's death, he was only dimly aware (at most) of the existence of the atom bomb and the contents of postwar plans.

## The Modern Vice Presidency

Truman's unpreparedness in 1945—and the rapid development of a cold war between the United States and the Soviet Union and the proliferation of nuclear-armed intercontinental ballistic missiles—increased public concern about the vice presidency. It became clear that the vice presidency should be held by leaders who were not just willing but ready and able to step into the presidency at a moment's notice. The heightened public concern has had consequences for vice presidential selection, activity, succession, and political status.

### Selection

To meet the new public expectations about vice presidential competence, most modern presidential candidates have paid considerable attention to experience, ability, and political compatibility in selecting their running mates. (Those who have not done so usually have suffered during the campaign as a result.) Winning votes on election day is still the goal, but presidential nominees realize that voters now care more about a vice presidential candidate's competence and loyalty—the ability to succeed to the presidency ably and to carry on the departed president's policies faithfully—than they do about having all regions of the country or factions of the party represented on the ticket. This realization has helped to create a climate for a stronger vice presidency. As Joel Goldstein has shown, the president is more likely to assign responsibilities to the vice president when the two are personally and politically compatible and when the president believes that the vice president has talents the administration needs.[16] These conditions frequently are met, as in the case of the three most recent administrations, as a consequence of the new selection criteria.

A concern for competence and loyalty in the vice presidency also characterized the solution Congress invented for a recurring problem of the executive that the challenges of the postwar era had made seem urgent: vice presidential vacancies. The Twenty-fifth Amendment, which established a procedure for selecting vice presidents in unusual circumstances, was passed in 1965 and ratified in 1967. Until then, the vice presidency had been vacant for parts of sixteen administrations, leaving the president without a constitutionally designated successor. The amendment authorized the president to fill vacancies in the vice presidency by appointment, with the advice and consent of both houses of Congress. The new procedure came in handy, albeit in circumstances its authors scarcely had imagined, in 1973, when Spiro T. Agnew resigned as vice president and was replaced by Gerald Ford, and in 1974, when Ford became president after President Richard M. Nixon resigned and appointed Nelson A. Rockefeller to fill the vacated vice presidency.

### Activity

One thing modern presidents do to reassure the nation that vice presidents are prepared to succeed to the presidency is to keep them informed about matters of state. As President Dwight D. Eisenhower's remark at a news conference indicates, to do otherwise would invite public criticism: "Even if Mr. Nixon and I were not good friends, I would still have him in every important conference of government, so that if the grim reaper would find it time to remove me from the scene, he is ready to step in without any interruption."[17] In 1949, at President Truman's initiative, the vice president was made a statutory member of the National Security Council. Vice presidents also receive national security briefings as a matter of course.

As a further means of reassurance, most presidents now encourage the vice president to stay active and in the public eye. Since Garner began the practice, vice presidents have traveled abroad on the president's behalf both with growing frequency—Nixon made seven foreign trips, Hubert H. Humphrey twelve, Walter F. Mondale fourteen, George Bush (during the first term) twenty[18]—and in pursuit of a wide variety of diplomatic missions, ranging from simple expressions of American goodwill to actual negotiations. Vice presidents since Garner also have met regularly with the cabinet and have served, to some degree, as a legislative liaison from the president to Congress—counting votes on Capitol Hill, lobbying discreetly, and listening to complaints and suggestions.

Alben W. Barkley, who served as vice president in the Truman administration, elevated the ceremonial duties of the vice presidency to center stage. Some of these, like crowning beauty queens (a Barkley favorite), are inconsequential, but others, such as commencement addresses and appearances at events that symbolize administration goals, need not be. Nixon, whose president did not enjoy partisan politics, carved out new vice presidential responsibilities that were as insignificant as commission chair and as important as public advocate of the administration's policies, leadership, and party. The advocacy role exposed the vice president to a wide range of audiences, including interest groups, party activists, journalists, and the general public.

During the 1960s and 1970s, vice presidents began to accumulate greater institutional resources to help them fulfill their more extensive duties. Lyndon Johnson, under President John F. Kennedy, gained for the vice presidency an impressive suite of offices in the Executive Office Building, adjacent to the White House; Agnew won a line item in the executive budget—between them they freed vice presidents from their earlier dependence on Congress for office space and operating funds. Even more significant institutional gains were registered by Ford and Rockefeller, the two vice presidents who were appointed under the Twenty-fifth Amendment and whose agreements to serve were urgently required by their presidents for political reasons. Ford, who feared becoming too dependent on a president who might well be removed from office, persuaded Nixon to increase dramatically his budget for hiring staff. The new personnel included support staff for press relations, speechmaking, scheduling, and administration (which meant the vice president no longer had to rely on the often unreliable White House for those functions), policy staff (enabling the vice president to develop useful advice on matters of presidential concern), and political staff (to help the vice president who had presidential ambitions to pursue them). Rockefeller secured a weekly place on the president's calendar for a private meeting.[19] He also enhanced the perquisites of the vice presidency—everything from a better airplane to serve as Air Force Two to an official residence (the old Naval Observatory) and a redesigned seal for the office. (The old seal showed an eagle at rest, the new one an eagle at full wingspread with a claw full of arrows and a starburst at its head.)

The vice presidency came into full flower during Mondale's tenure in the administration of President Jimmy Carter. As a candidate in 1976, Mondale participated in the first nationally televised debate between the vice presidential candidates. His most tangible contributions to the institution during his term as vice president, building on earlier gains, were the authorization he won to attend all presidential meetings, full access to the flow of papers to and from the president, and an office in the west wing of the White House. More important, perhaps, was that Mondale demonstrated that the vice president could serve the president (who, in Mondale's case, had selected him with unprecedented care and attention) as a valued adviser on virtually all matters of politics and public policy, whereas previously vice presidents had been consulted by their superiors mainly on those matters in which they were thought to have expertise—for example, Johnson on space issues, Humphrey on civil rights, and Rockefeller on domestic policy.

George Bush, as vice president to President Ronald Reagan, was heir to all the institutional gains in both roles and resources that his recent predecessors had won. Although he did not enter office enjoying the same sort of close personal relationship with Reagan that Mondale had with Carter, Bush worked hard and, for the most part, successfully to win the president's confidence. As Bush realized, the degree to which the new activities of the vice presidency translate into real influence within the White House still depends in large part on the president's perception of the vice president's ability, energy, and, perhaps most important, loyalty. But, because of the new vice presidential selection criteria, this perception is more likely to be favorable than at any previous time in history. And, because of the institutionalization of numerous roles and resources in the vice presidency, the vice president has a greater opportunity than ever to be of real service to the president.

## Succession and Disability

In addition to creating a procedure to fill vice presidential vacancies, the Twenty-fifth Amendment accomplished two other purposes. One was to state explicitly the right of a successor vice president to assume the office of president and to serve for the remainder of the departed president's term, an uncontroversial measure that conferred constitutional sanction on a long-established precedent. The other was to establish a set of procedures to handle the problem of presidential disability. The vice president was to be involved not only as the recipient of the powers and duties of the presidency (not the office itself) during times of presidential disability, but as the essential figure in any effort to remove governing responsibility from a president who was unable or unwilling to acknowledge a disability. This grant of power, however, has been more illusory than real. For fear of seeming unduly aggressive or ambitious, vice presidents have bent over backwards to avoid disability determinations, ceding effective control of the problem to the White House staff.

*Political Status*

The modern vice presidency enjoys a curious political status. No incumbent vice president has been elected president since 1836, when Martin Van Buren accomplished the feat. Yet, in a marked departure from previous political history, the greater talent and higher visibility of modern vice presidents typically have made them front-runners for their party's presidential nomination. The Twenty-second Amendment, which became part of the Constitution in 1951, also helps in some cases: by limiting presidents to two terms, it frees the vice president who serves in a second-term administration to step forward as a presidential candidate, as Nixon did in 1960 and Bush in 1988, without fear of unduly alienating the president. Of the recent vice presidents, Nixon, Humphrey, Mondale, and Bush were nominated directly for president, and Truman, Johnson, and Ford were nominated for full terms after succeeding to the presidency; Barkley, Agnew, and Rockefeller did not actively seek a presidential nomination.

## Conclusion

The curious political status of the vice presidency is a reminder that, for all its progress as an institution, some qualities of the office endure. Although new selection criteria make the nomination of vice presidential candidates who are competent to be president more likely, the recent examples of William E. Miller in 1964, Agnew in 1968 and 1972, Thomas F. Eagleton in 1972, and Geraldine A. Ferraro in 1984 indicate that older forms of ticket balancing are not yet extinct. New selection criteria may foster greater harmony in office between president and vice president, but they do not guarantee it. (Perhaps it is not surprising that the two modern presidents who some say inflicted the greatest pain on their vice presidents, Johnson and Nixon, had been vice presidents themselves.)[20] Finally, although vice presidents enjoy more resources, responsibilities, and influence than ever before, they do so mainly at the sufferance of the president. The price of power for a vice president can be high—unflagging loyalty, sublimation of one's own views and ambitions, and receptiveness to the president's beck and call. In a twist of irony, the very devotion to the president that wins the vice president kudos among fellow partisans may invite rejection by the broader electorate in the general election; the voters may regard the vice president as lacking the independent character and vision they seek in their presidents.

# Chapter 3
# Selection

$\mathbf{M}$ost students and practitioners of American politics agree, as a matter of principle, that vice presidents should be chosen with their constitutional role as presidential successor uppermost in mind. To the extent that this belief is taken seriously, it implies two "governance" criteria for evaluating the vice presidential selection process and any proposals to alter it. One is the competence of nominees to be president. Historically, six of nine presidential successions have occurred during the vice president's first year in office, suggesting that even the best on-the-job training is no substitute for a wise initial selection. The second criterion is loyalty to the policies of the president or presidential candidate, so that some measure of continuity in government is likely to be maintained after a succession.

In practice, governance criteria for vice presidential selection may or may not conflict with constitutional and democratic values that the public prizes. This is a fundamentally important "legitimacy" criterion, and it has been the source, for example, of much debate about the right of nominees for president to select vice presidential running mates on their own. Governance criteria also may or may not accord with the operation of the two "election" criteria that traditionally have dominated the process of choosing vice presidents. The first, and the more important, election criterion is that the vice presidential nomination broaden the presidential candidate's appeal in the general election. The second, also significant mainly for its effect on the ticket's chances in the election, is that it unite the party in the aftermath of the presidential nominating contest.

The ideal vice presidential selection process would fulfill the governance and legitimacy criteria and would accommodate the election criteria. Stated more plainly, the process would foster the selection of competent and loyal vice presidents by constitutional and democratic means while helping parties to unite and presidential candidates to win the general election.

All this mixing and matching of governance, legitimacy, and election criteria is complicated enough when applied to the usual method of vice presidential selection—nomination by the parties and election by the electoral college. But the laws and Constitution of the United States and the rules of the two major parties also provide three methods of unusual selection. If the vice presidency becomes vacant, the Twenty-fifth Amendment requires the president to appoint a new vice president and obtain congressional confirmation of the nominee. If a vice presidential candidate leaves the ticket before the election, each party's rules stipulate that its national committee will choose a replacement. Finally, if no candidate for vice president receives a majority of electoral votes, the Senate is empowered by the Twelfth Amendment to choose a vice president from the two candidates who receive the greatest number of electoral votes.

## Usual Selection

During the nineteenth and early twentieth centuries, party leaders, not presidential candidates, chose the parties' nominees for vice president. In order to take the outcome of the convention's presidential nominating contest into account, they selected the vice presidential nominee right afterward. Election criteria, applied in a setting that encouraged haste, invariably drove their decisions. Vice presidential nominations were used almost exclusively to balance the ticket, partly to heal the party's divisions, partly to win additional support in the general election, if only in one large state. (From 1900 to 1920, five politicians from Indiana and four from New York won vice presidential nominations because those were two of the very few large competitive states in the country at that time.) If elected, the vice president could look forward to being replaced at the next convention, when, in an altered political setting, election criteria were likely to mandate the choice of a different vice presidential candidate who could provide the ticket with a new set of electoral balances. Until 1912, when James S. Sherman was chosen to run again with William Howard Taft, no vice president was nominated for reelection by a party convention.

Not only were governance criteria neglected in this procedure, the extreme application of election criteria actively discouraged competence and loyalty in the vice presidency. Ticket balancing as then practiced usually paired candidates from different and often opposing factions of the party—North-South, hard money-soft money, Stalwart-Progressive, and the like. Seldom did the vice president feel much affinity for the president, or the president much trust for the vice president, after the election. The prospect of being replaced at the end of the term dissuaded talented political leaders from accepting vice presidential nominations in the first place. Politicians who hoped someday to be elected president shunned the office; except for Martin Van Buren in 1836, no nineteenth-century vice president was nominated for president by a convention, not even those who succeeded to the presidency when the president died.

The first modification in the vice presidential selection process came early in the twentieth century, with the vice presidency of Theodore Roosevelt. The rise of national news media made vice presidents more visible; a new style of active electioneering made them more popular and better established among party activists. Although election criteria still determined each vice presidential nomination, they now were applied a little differently. Within the party, the price of dropping a vice president from the ticket became too high: in this century, no vice president has been denied the chance to run again when an incumbent president sought a second term. Governance criteria continued to be ignored, but at least competent politicians were not discouraged from accepting vice presidential nominations by the promise of a humiliating dismissal four years later. It remained unusual during the early twentieth century, but no longer was unheard of, for a leader of stature like Charles Dawes, Charles Curtis, or John Nance Garner to accept the second spot on the ticket.

An even more significant alteration in vice presidential selection came in 1940, when Franklin D. Roosevelt seized from party leaders the right to choose his running mate. Roosevelt had long felt that the president should put the vice president to use in the administration— he had written an article to that effect while running for vice president in 1920—and entrusted more responsibility to his first vice president, Garner, than has any president since George Washington. But Roosevelt and the conservative Garner (whom party leaders had placed on the ticket in 1932) had a falling out in 1937, which convinced the president that he had to pick his own vice president if he were to use the office as he desired.

Roosevelt accomplished his goal by threatening to refuse the convention's nomination for a third term as president if it rejected his choice for vice president, Henry A. Wallace.[1] Although the circumstances of Roosevelt's precedent-setting power grab—his extraordinary standing in the party and unrivaled concern for the vice presidency as an office— were unusual, the transfer of the effective power to select vice presidential candidates from party leaders to presidential nominees probably was bound to occur eventually, as part of the more general rise of the twentieth-century presidency as a political institution and the simultaneous decline of parties.

Harry S. Truman's woefully unprepared succession to the presidency in 1945 was the source of further changes in the vice presidential selection process, mainly in response to heightened public concern about the ability of vice presidents in the nuclear age to fulfill their successor role ably and faithfully. By indicating that they valued standards of competence and loyalty in vice presidential selection, the public—political journalists, scholars, activists, and voters—helped to bring these governance criteria into conformity with at least the more important of the two election criteria, namely, winning the election.

The fruits of the new emphasis on governance criteria can be seen in the roster of postwar vice presidential nominees. The postwar era has been marked by an almost complete absence of ideologically opposed running mates, and those vice presidential candidates who have differed even slightly on the issues with the heads of their tickets (as George Bush, who once described Ronald Reagan's supply-side tax proposals as "voodoo economics," did in 1980) have hastened to gloss over past disagreements and deny that any exist in the present. The record is still more compelling with regard to competence. From 1948 to 1984, the vice presidential candidate as often as not has been the more experienced member of the ticket in high government office, including John Sparkman in 1952, Estes Kefauver in 1956, Lyndon B. Johnson and Henry Cabot Lodge in 1960, and Walter F. Mondale in 1976. Around half the vice presidential nominees in this period already had sought or been prominently mentioned for the presidency at the time they were picked, and the majority of them later ran for their party's presidential nomination, often successfully.[2]

Not much is left to chance in modern vice presidential selection, at least not when the presidential nominating contest is settled, as is typical nowadays, well in advance of the convention. Jimmy Carter set a precedent in 1976 when he conducted a careful, organized preconvention search for a running mate. From a list of four hundred Democratic officeholders that aides compiled for him in April, he narrowed the pool of contenders to fourteen. Pollster Patrick Caddell tested their relative electoral strengths, and aide Charles Kirbo interviewed several of them. Prospective nominees were asked to fill out questionnaires, answering detailed inquiries about their finances, health, and personal and political lives. Carter interviewed the seven finalists in July and finally tapped Mondale at the convention. Mondale followed a similar procedure as the Democratic presidential candidate in 1984. Reagan did nothing so elaborate in 1980 because he hoped to lure former president Gerald R. Ford onto the ticket, but he and his aides did give considerable thought to the kind of running mate they wanted.

Thus, in each of the three most recent instances in which a vice presidential nomination had to be decided, the presidential candidate undertook a search well designed to yield a reasoned, responsible selection sensitive to the public desire for a worthy presidential successor. Public-spiritedness may account in part for their having done so, but a more likely explanation is that they realized that the presidential candidate who pays insufficient attention to governance criteria in choosing the vice presidential nominee will suffer for it in the election. A recent study indicates that, in the general election campaign, vice presidential candidates are most likely to make the front page for bad things, such as scandals or blunders.[3] To select a running mate whose competence and loyalty are less than certain is to invite such coverage. It also is to hand the other party a potent issue. A Democratic commercial in 1968 displayed the words "Agnew for Vice President?" over a soundtrack of rising laughter. The spot ended with a voice intoning, "This would be funny if it weren't so serious." In 1976, a Carter ad showed pictures of Mondale and Robert A. Dole, the Republican vice presidential nominee, then asked, "When you know that four of the last six vice presidents have wound up being president, who would you like to see a heartbeat away from the presidency? Hmmm?" Differences in the qualifications of the candidates are also likely to appear quite clearly in the vice presidential debate, televised on all networks, that now is a part of most presidential campaigns. Ultimately, the price of slighting governance criteria when choosing a running mate is votes: surveys from various elections indicate that a poor vice presidential candidate can harm a ticket's chances on election day.[4]

In sum, in recent times a concern for competence and loyalty, the main governance criteria for choosing vice presidential candidates, has not so much displaced as come into harmony with the main election criterion, that of winning the general election. Governance criteria even can accommodate, at least, some traditional forms of ticket balancing that still are practiced. Specifically, Protestant presidential candidates often choose Catholic running mates, candidates without extensive experience in the federal government usually pair themselves with Washington insiders, and presidential candidates typically limit their choice for a vice president to political leaders from the other parts of the country.[5]

There is, to be sure, no guarantee that governance criteria will be satisfied in every nomination of a vice presidential candidate. Four sets of circumstances may impede such a choice. First, politicians do not always see their interests clearly. Richard M. Nixon was too clever by half when, acting on the theory that a relatively unknown running mate would have few enemies and cost the ticket few votes, he chose Agnew in 1968. A second, more serious problem is that one election criterion—uniting the party—continues to bear little relation to the governance criteria for vice presidential selection. Threats from the National Organization for Women and other feminist groups to oppose a male nominee for vice president at the 1984 Democratic convention forced Mondale's hand—he feared that with a fractured party he had no hope of winning the general election. It is hard to imagine that Mondale would have picked any other third-term member of the House of Representatives without notable foreign affairs experience than Geraldine A. Ferraro. Third, conventions still select the candidate for vice president within hours of the presidential nomination. A presidential nominating contest that is unresolved going into the convention, like the George McGovern-Hubert H. Humphrey battle in 1972 or the Ford-Reagan race in 1976, tends to consume the time and attention of the candidates, making a hasty choice of a running mate in an atmosphere of frenzy and exhaustion all too likely. Finally, party leaders can make it difficult for a president even to consider removing a vice president they especially like, such as Nixon in 1956 or Agnew in 1972.

### Suggested Reforms

The selection process is a frequent target of reform among students of the vice presidency. Some critics worry not so much about the criteria presidential candidates apply when choosing their running mates as about the haste and pressure with which they make their choices, conditions that may distort their judgment. Others seek wider public participation in the selection process, believing both that the legitimacy criterion of democratic choice is violated by the current process of de facto presidential designation and that at least one governance criterion, vice presidential competence, would be better served by letting voters participate in the decision. Finally, some critics are convinced that election criteria—uniting the party and winning votes for the ticket—are inherently in conflict with the governance criteria of competence and loyalty. A number of them have proposed that all vice presidents be appointed, using the procedures described in Section 2 of the Twenty-fifth Amendment.

*Haste.* The traditional order of business at the national nominating convention provides for the vice presidential candidate to be selected the evening after the presidential candidate is chosen. In practice, the nominee for president is expected to announce a recommendation no later than the afternoon of the vice presidential nomination, which reduces the interval to about half a day. To some reformers, this schedule conjures up images—sometimes drawn from experience—of exhausted and emotionally drained presidential candidates meeting into the wee hours of the morning with equally frazzled advisers, trying desperately to make an intelligent decision about a matter that they are concentrating on for the first time, and, all too often, failing in that effort.[6]

A number of proposals have been made to remedy the problem of haste. Varied as they are, each would prolong the vice presidential selection process by injecting more time—some before, others during, still others after the convention. A number of commissions—including the Democratic party's Vice Presidential Selection Committee, which was chaired by former vice president Humphrey in 1973, the 1976 Study Group on Vice Presidential Selection of the John F. Kennedy School of Government at Harvard University, and the American Bar Association's Special Committee on Electoral Reform, which also met in 1976—have suggested that candidates who are seeking a party's presidential nomination be required or encouraged to release for public scrutiny, in advance of the convention, the names of those they are considering as running mates.[7] The Democrats' experience with Thomas Eagleton was fresh in the minds of these reformers. (George McGovern had tapped Eagleton as his running mate in 1972, only to find out later from press reports that he had once undergone electric shock treatments for mental illness.) By releasing names in advance, reformers believed, the problems a prospective vice presidential nominee might present could be identified before it was too late.

Other proposals born of concern about haste would modify the convention itself, usually by inserting a day between the presidential and vice presidential nominations. This could be done within the bounds of the customary four-day convention by reversing the order in which the party platform is adopted and the presidential candidate nominated. (The revised order would be: presidential nomination on the second day, platform on the third day, vice presidential nomination on the fourth day.) Or the traditional order could be maintained but with an "off" day added after the nomination for president. Finally, some have suggested that the convention adjourn without nominating a vice presidential candidate, allowing the presidential nominee to present a choice to the party's national committee within a designated period. The Humphrey commission proposed that national committee selection, which was used to nominate Sargent Shriver for vice president in 1972 after Eagleton resigned from the ticket, be made an option the presidential candidate could ask to use, pending the convention's approval.

*Wider participation.* A number of individuals have worried that the current system of vice presidential selection gives too much power to the presidential nominee, whom they fear will wield it solely to increase the chances of winning the general election, with governance criteria shunted aside. Their express purpose for seeking a change is to make the process more democratic and thus, they argue, more legitimate and more effective.

Some would broaden participation in the nominating of vice presidential candidates by allowing the electorate a direct role. One such idea, which could be accommodated within the current system, would be to require presidential candidates to designate their running mates before the start of the primary season, so that voters could choose among complete tickets. In 1976, Reagan, desperate to halt President Ford's march to the nomination, announced the name of his candidate for vice president weeks in advance of the Republican convention and moved that the convention require Ford to do the same before the presidential balloting began. Reagan's motion failed; in any event, his own announcement did not come until after the primaries were over. A somewhat different proposal would urge states to hold separate but simultaneous presidential and vice presidential primaries or caucuses, leading to a convention nomination for vice president that is independent of the presidential nomination. Under such an arrangement, candidates would run for vice president as they do now for president. A third suggestion for wider voter participation is more radical in form but conservative in spirit. In an effort to approximate the original constitutional ideal that the vice president should be the second-most qualified person to be president, it would create a national primary for each party in which voters would cast two ballots for president, with the runner-up winning the vice presidential nomination.[8]

Another strategy to broaden participation in the vice presidential selection process would be to turn the decision over to the convention, giving party activists a role. The Democratic presidential nominee in 1956, Adlai Stevenson, elected to do so; the convention chose Estes Kefauver for vice president after a spirited contest. Some proponents of this idea would have the presidential nominee structure the convention's decision by offering it three or four acceptable choices and letting the delegates decide among them.[9]

*Appoint the vice president.* The process created by the Twenty-fifth Amendment to fill vice presidential vacancies, and the nation's experiences with it in 1973 and 1974, impressed some reformers so deeply that they would redefine the vice presidency as an appointive office. Conventions no longer would nominate and the electoral college no longer would select vice presidents under their proposal. Instead, the president-elect would nominate a vice president, and both houses of Congress, voting separately, would confirm the nomination.

Supporters of an appointive vice presidency offer several arguments in defense of their idea. By removing vice presidential selection from the electoral process, they claim, their proposal would end any conflict between election criteria for vice presidential selection and governance criteria. Nor would the legitimacy criterion be violated because people really do not vote for vice president anyway. (Indeed, the new system would be as democratic as the current one, in which the president chooses and a representative body—the party convention—confirms the nomination.) An appointive vice presidency would draw from a broader talent pool, the case continues, because some leaders who would be excellent successors to the presidency are not willing to run for vice president in an election campaign. Finally, haste no longer would characterize the selection of vice presidents. The president could make a nomination, and Congress could review it, deliberately.[10]

### Discussion

Each of the suggested reforms of the vice presidential selection process has flaws to match the virtues its proponents celebrate. With regard to haste, for example, to postpone nomination of the vice presidential candidate for one day seems trivial; to delay it until after the convention would deny the party the opportunity to leave the convention with its business complete, united and undistracted by any concern other than winning the election.

Most of the proposals to increase voter participation, notably vice presidential primaries and a national primary, bar the presidential nominee from any formal role in designating the vice president, which would undermine the chances for cooperation in office or a faithful succession. Requiring presidential candidates to announce their running mates at the start of the primary season would replace this problem with another: it would reduce the talent pool for vice president by excluding candidates for president. (The vice presidential primaries proposal also would exclude presidential candidates from consideration.)

Suggestions to widen the convention's participation in the nomination of vice presidents have limitations of their own. A truly open floor fight could produce a vice presidential candidate whom the presidential nominee does not want. In office, such a vice president might feel entitled to act independently or even oppose the president. Allowing the presidential nominee to limit the convention's choice to a few designated candidates would mitigate these problems. But it also would eliminate political leaders who would be willing to accept a vice presidential nomination but not be willing to fight for one and would alienate some who were left off the list of three or four. Finally, what are presidential nominees to do if, as usually is the case, they have a clear first choice for a running mate: Conceal their preference and run the risk of having to accept a less happy alternative? Stack the deck with unpalatable candidates so that the preferred nominee will stand out as the only reasonable selection? A process that invites its own undermining also invites cynicism.

As for the appointive vice president idea, it is as flawed in some ways as it is seductive in others. It would distract the president and tie up Congress at the start of the new administration, when policy development should be the foremost concern. It would encourage the appointment of a bland political figure, so as not to embroil the president in a nasty fight early in his administration. It would subvert the Twentieth Amendment, which assumes the existence of a vice-president-elect to act as successor if the president-elect is unable to be inaugurated as president. It probably would not work as intended in practice: public pressure on the presidential candidates to reveal their preferences for vice president in advance of the election would be intense. And although an appointive vice president might well violate the forms of democratic control more than the substance, form is important in matters of legitimacy.

Finally, if each proposal to change the vice presidential selection process has limitations of its own, together they share two common problems. The first, and more important, is the relative mildness of the pathology they seek to cure. The current system may be less in need of reform than at any time in the history of the vice presidency. To be sure, the selection of vice presidents who, if called upon, would be worthy successors to the presidency is the standard against which any process should be judged. But the governance criteria that accord with this standard—competence and loyalty—still are subordinate in practice to the election criteria that traditionally have dominated vice presidential nominations, namely, uniting the party and winning votes for the ticket. Fortunately, the public, ever more aware of the need for successor presidents who can fill the office ably and faithfully, has taught politicians that they cannot increase their chances to win the election except by applying governance criteria to the selection of vice presidential candidates.

A second common failing of almost all the remedies for what ails the vice presidential selection process is that they are all ill-suited or at best irrelevant to the renomination of incumbent vice presidents. This is not surprising, considering that the reforms invariably were invented in reaction to some poor initial nomination for vice president. But what need is there for more or different primaries, a prolonged convention, or a postelection appointment process when a vice president is simply to be renominated?

Partly because political leaders know that the public is watching, and partly because the modern presidential nominating process tends to produce early victors, haste and closed participation in vice presidential selection have diminished in recent years. When the presidential nomination is effectively decided well in advance of the convention, the winning candidate has both the opportunity and the incentive to devote considerable time, attention, and resources to the choice of a running mate. It is now standard practice for the names of those being considered for vice president either to be leaked to the press or, as in 1976 and 1984, openly announced. There is ample time for public and party expressions of enthusiasm or scorn to be offered about the prospective nominees. Investigations of their backgrounds can go forward.

Difficulties remain in the vice presidential selection process. But they can be better dealt with by simple actions than by the proposals made by reformers to date. Hasty, secretive nominations still are all too likely when the presidential contest lasts into the convention, which still happens on occasion. But such pressured choices need not occur. Journalists, activists, and voters can force presidential candidates to think about the vice presidency throughout the campaign by persistently asking them by what process and with what criteria they intend to fill it. Another remaining difficulty is that one election criterion—uniting the party— still may impede the selection of worthy presidential successors. The conflict is not inherent—not all, probably not most, political leaders whose nomination for vice president would help to heal a party are incompetent or disloyal. Nor is uniting the party a criterion without merit— to the extent that the American political system requires healthy political parties, anything that encourages party unity is much to be prized. And, of course, should factions in a party take matters to an extreme and make representation on the ticket the price of unity, even at the expense of competence or loyalty, voters can have the final say at the polls.

## Unusual Selection

Since the early formation of political parties, the passage of the Twelfth Amendment, and the invention of national nominating conventions, the usual method of vice presidential selection—party nomination and election by the electoral college—have been adequate to the task in the great majority of cases. On five occasions, however, unusual selection methods have had to be employed: twice when the vice president was appointed under Section 2 of the Twenty-fifth Amendment, once when the Senate elected the vice president, and twice when a vice presidential candidate was nominated by a party's national committee to fill a vacancy on the ticket. All of these methods still are available for use. None is wholly unproblematic.

### Amendment XXV, Section 2

No provision was made in the original Constitution to fill vacancies in the vice presidency. Even as late as 1947, when the nation had been left without a vice president during parts of almost half its first thirty-three presidencies (by fourteen presidential and vice presidential deaths and one vice presidential resignation), the relatively low status of the vice presidency meant there was little sense of urgency about vice presidential vacancies. (The nation's good fortune in never having lost a successor president contributed to that sense of complacency.) Congress that year simply rewrote the presidential succession law to provide that, in the absence of a vice president, the Speaker of the House and the president pro tempore of the Senate would be next in line to the presidency.

Congress finally dealt with the vacant vice presidency in 1965. The rise in public anxiety about the office that occurred during the postwar era had helped to create a general climate of concern by then, but there were two more immediate spurs to action. The assassination of President John F. Kennedy left the nation with a president, Lyndon Johnson, who had a history of heart trouble and whose designated successors were an old and ailing speaker, John W. McCormack, and, as Senate president, an even older and iller Carl Hayden. In addition, President Eisenhower's various illnesses in the 1950s had prodded Congress to address the presidential disability issue, and it was clear that whatever solution it developed would rely on the participation and presence of a vice president.

Congress considered a number of proposals about how to fill vice presidential vacancies. Some would have made Congress the selecting body, empowering it to choose the vice president either completely on its own, subject to presidential veto, or from a list submitted by the president. Truman's widely expressed belief that presidents should not be allowed to appoint their own successors, which had helped persuade Congress in 1947 to make the speaker, not, as in the past, the secretary of state, second in line to the presidency, provided a strong argument for these proposals. But congressional selection ultimately was rejected for its potentially corrosive effects on administration unity (these effects were seen as harmful in general and perilous in view of the role Congress was about to assign the vice president in matters of presidential disability). Another proposal, offered by former vice president Nixon, would have left out Congress entirely, for fear that, if controlled by the opposition party, it might obstruct the president for partisan reasons. Nixon suggested that the president nominate a vice president for confirmation by the electoral college of the most recent election, since it had chosen the original vice president. The fatal flaw in this proposal was that the electoral college is not a deliberative or investigative body—or any kind of body at all, considering that it never meets. Finally, some would simply have left the status quo unaltered, convinced that any method of vice presidential appointment would be so damaging to the Constitution's mandate that the president and vice president "be elected" that the 1947 law providing for succession by the speaker should be left to stand.[11]

In the end, Congress determined that "whenever there is a vacancy in the office of the Vice President, the President shall nominate a Vice

President who shall take office upon confirmation of a majority vote of both Houses of Congress." Section 2 of the Twenty-fifth Amendment, it was felt, would meet the governance criteria for vice presidential selection because it left the primary responsibility to the president and was divorced from electoral politics. It would meet the legitimacy criterion because it was familiar, operating in the spirit both of other constitutional appointments and of the usual process for choosing vice presidents, in which the presidential candidate nominates and the convention confirms.

In enacting the Twenty-fifth Amendment, Congress seems to have assumed that death (either the president's or the vice president's) typically would produce the vice presidential vacancies that activate the selection provision, as had happened in all but one of the sixteen previous cases. (The exception was Vice President John C. Calhoun's resignation in 1831.) But in 1973, Vice President Agnew resigned as part of a plea bargain that enabled him to avoid prosecution on political corruption charges, and President Nixon and a Democratic Congress used their new constitutional power to make House Republican leader Gerald Ford vice president. Less than a year later, Nixon resigned rather than undergo an impeachment trial. When Ford succeeded to the presidency, the vice presidency was vacant once more. Ford nominated former New York governor Nelson A. Rockefeller, and Congress again approved.

*Remaining Concerns.* Neither the enactment of Section 2 of the Twenty-fifth Amendment nor the nation's two experiences with it have ended debate about the filling of vice presidential vacancies. Some criticisms, based on the Ford and Rockefeller nominations, are procedural; others, more long-standing, are fundamental.

Most of the procedural concerns involve the confirmation process in Congress. At Congress's request, both Ford and Rockefeller underwent extensive background checks by the Federal Bureau of Investigation; congressional hearings and debates also were lengthy. In all, Ford's confirmation took nearly two months; Rockefeller's four. In view of the amendment's original rationale, which was to have a vice president available at all times for succession or disability, any substantial procedural delay is self-defeating. At one time, Congress had considered stipulating a thirty-day limit in the amendment, but decided that it should allow for unusually difficult nominations that would require more time. Yet neither the Ford nor Rockefeller nominations posed any special problems. Thus, one proposed reform would set a generous but firm limit of ninety days. If Congress failed to act within that time, the nomination would be considered approved.[12]

Another procedural concern about Section 2 is the absence of widely accepted criteria for congressional evaluation. Is profound disagreement with a nominee's policy views a suitable basis for rejection, as in an ordinary election? Or, at the opposite extreme, is the president entitled to relatively complete deference, unless there is serious concern about the nominee's integrity or competence, as with most cabinet appointments? The answer probably lies somewhere in between, but the wide-ranging Ford and Rockefeller confirmation hearings indicated profound uncertainty about where that middle ground should be.[13]

Some critics' objections to Section 2 involve basic issues of legitimacy and governance. By one reading, the Ford and Rockefeller experiences were encouraging: the United States was led during its bicentennial year by an appointed president and an appointed vice president, with no serious objections raised to their right to rule. Yet in 1976, Ford became the first successor president in this century not to be elected to a term in his own right, and Rockefeller was not even nominated by his party.

The Ford and Rockefeller experiences also serve as a reminder that one of the properties of Section 2 is to allow an endless string of appointed presidents and vice presidents. Even if the idea of an elected president appointing a vice president is regarded as legitimate, doubts may arise about the appropriateness of having an appointed vice-president-turned-president appoint the new successor. By this reckoning, Nixon's nomination of Ford was more acceptable than Ford's nomination of Rockefeller. It may be that no more than one exercise of Section 2 should be allowed in any four-year term. Any subsequent vice presidential vacancy would be left unfilled, with the Speaker of the House standing as successor.

Another fundamental criticism of the appointive vice presidency is that the president will feel compelled to fill a vacancy with a "respectable, pallid choice."[14] To appoint a vice president of presidential caliber is, perversely, to risk rousing resentment among politicians in both parties. Members of Congress from the opposition party may be reluctant to confirm (and thus create) a possible opponent in the next presidential election; legislators of the president's party with White House ambitions of their own may be even more hesitant to do so. Political self-interest could prevent the president from appointing certain eminently qualified nominees and subject the nominee who is selected to pressure from Congress to forswear any presidential ambitions.

*Senate Election I: Living Candidates*

The Constitution provides that if no nominee for vice president receives a majority of electoral votes, the Senate shall elect one of the two vice presidential candidates with the highest number of electoral votes. Such an election has occurred only once. In 1836, the Democratic party's presidential nominee, Martin Van Buren, received a majority of electoral votes, but his running mate, Richard M. Johnson, fell one short when Virginia's twenty-three Democratic electors, disapproving of Johnson's dalliances with a succession of slave mistresses, denied him their support. The Senate elected Johnson quickly, 33-16, but the straight party nature of the vote leaves one to wonder what would have happened if the opposition party had controlled the Senate. No protocol exists for such a situation; indeed, should it arise again, senators who believe that their party's candidate for vice president is being treated unfairly could boycott the proceedings, which in most cases would deny the Senate the two-thirds quorum that is constitutionally required for it to elect.

An 1836-style Senate vice presidential election conceivably could be triggered by, say, a serious scandal involving the winning vice presidential candidate that occurred or was revealed between the first Tuesday after the first Monday in November, when the electors are chosen, and the first Monday after the second Wednesday in December, when they vote. No law effectively binds electors to vote in a particular way.

More likely, however, the occasion for a Senate election would arise if a third-party ticket prevented either major party from winning a majority of electoral votes. Under the Twelfth Amendment, while the Senate, assuming a quorum, was choosing between the two leading vice presidential candidates by simple majority vote (a process well designed to produce a winner in most cases), the House would be voting for president by a much more complicated procedure. In the House, not only would the three highest electoral vote recipients be considered, but the support of a majority of state delegations is required for election, with evenly divided delegations casting no votes. Thus, Twelfth Amendment procedures might well produce a vice president but no president by Inauguration Day, in which case the vice president would serve as acting president until the House reached a decision. If the House were hopelessly deadlocked, the vice president conceivably could exercise the powers and duties of the presidency for the entire four-year term.

At root, this is a flaw of the Twelfth Amendment, not of the vice presidency. Direct popular election, with the voters choosing among complete tickets, would eliminate the problem. So would a revision of the Constitution that could make it easier for the House to elect a president in the event of an electoral college deadlock or that converted the election of the president and the vice president into a single choice for electors and legislators, not separate ones.

### Senate Election II: Deceased Winning Candidate

Section 3 of the Twentieth Amendment provides that "if, at the time fixed for the beginning of the term of the President, the President elect shall have died, the Vice President elect shall become President." Should that occur, the Twenty-fifth Amendment then would cover the filling of the vacant vice presidency, as it would if the vice-president-elect were to die.

But what would happen if a presidential or vice presidential candidate who had received a majority when the electors voted in mid-December died or resigned before attaining "elect" status, which occurs only when Congress counts the votes on January 6?[15] Constitutionally, if a vice presidential candidate dies, Section 4 of the Twentieth Amendment applies:

> The Congress may by law provide for the case of the death of any of the persons from whom the House of Representatives may choose a President whenever the right of choice shall have devolved upon them, and for the case of the death of any of the persons from whom the Senate may choose a Vice President whenever the right of choice shall have devolved upon them.

But Congress has passed no such law. Thus, in counting the electoral votes on January 6, it would have to improvise. One course of action would be for Congress to declare that no candidate for vice president had received a majority of votes, in which case the Senate would have to choose the vice president. Since the Senate's choice is confined by the Twelfth Amendment to the two highest electoral vote recipients, its only alternatives would be to pick the opposition party nominee for vice president or to elect no one at all, which would violate the Constitution's instruction that the Senate "shall choose" and would leave the nation without a vice president for the next four years. The other course Congress could take would be to count the electoral votes and declare the dead vice presidential candidate elected. That would produce a more pleasing result—after the inauguration the president would pick a new vice president under the Twenty-fifth Amendment—but, as a procedure, it would fly in the face of both common sense and the Constitution's requirement that to be eligible for the vice presidency a person must be at least thirty-five years old, a citizen, and a resident—that is, alive.

Roughly the same set of problems would arise if a winning candidate for president were to die between mid-December and January 6. Clearly, under the Twentieth Amendment, the winning vice presidential candidate would be declared vice-president-elect. If Congress chose to count the deceased presidential candidate's electoral votes, the vice-president-elect would be inaugurated as president, then would invoke the Twenty-fifth Amendment to appoint a new vice president. But if Congress elected not to count the votes, the House—again because of Congress's failure to legislate under Section 4 of the Twentieth Amendment—would have to choose between the two living presidential candidates who had received the most electoral votes. Realistically, its choice would be to elect the defeated major-party nominee or make no selection at all. In the latter case, the vice president would serve as acting president for four years, with no one acting as vice president.

## Selection by the National Party

The rules of both major parties provide that, if a vacancy on the ticket occurs before the election, the national party is empowered to fill it. (Until 1988, both major parties authorized their national committees to make the choice; in 1988, the Democrats authorized their party's "super delgates" to do so.) Such a procedure is straightforward and uncontroversial when a vice presidential vacancy occurs prior to election day in November. As in 1972, when McGovern asked the Democratic National Committee to nominate Shriver for vice president, the public would almost certainly accept the legitimacy of the presidential candidate turning to the national committee as a proxy for the convention.

A somewhat different reaction might occur if the national committee nomination came between election day and the day in mid-December when the electors cast their votes. In 1912, the Republican vice presidential candidate, incumbent James S. Sherman, died on October 30. The Republican National Committee met after the election, which the Republicans lost overwhelmingly, and nominated Nicholas Murray Butler to receive Sherman's eight electoral votes for vice president. Butler's nomination was accepted without controversy, but certain broader questions remained unanswered. Would the public and its electors accept the right of the victorious national party in effect to name the vice president, even if the party simply confirmed the choice of the presidential candidate? If the winning presidential candidate died, would the winning vice presidential candidate be the presumptive replacement of the national party? If so, as seems likely, would the party then accept the former vice presidential candidate's choice of a new running mate? Would electors?

Questions such as these may do nothing more than underscore again the importance of using governance criteria for vice presidential selection, to assure that an able successor will be standing by even before the term begins. In any event, the right of national parties to fill vacancies on the ticket thus far has been wholly uncontroversial as an emergency arrangement. Indeed, some critics of the usual vice presidential selection process would prefer to make the party method standard practice.

## Conclusion

For all its imperfections, vice presidential selection has improved greatly in recent decades. The main goal of the selection process—namely, to choose vice presidents who, if needed, will be worthy successors to the presidency—is being achieved more successfully than at any time in history. The remaining problems are, for the most part, solvable, minor, or both.

### Usual Selection

To understand the reason why the process by which vice presidents usually are selected has improved is as important as to mark the improvement itself. It is not that politicians have put aside the election criteria—uniting the party and winning votes for the ticket— that traditionally have animated their vice presidential choices in order to accommodate the governance criteria—competence and loyalty—and the legitimacy criterion—constitutional and democratic values—that the rest of the political system prizes. It is rather that, ever since the importance of having an able and faithful vice president available to assume the presidency if needed became clear with the birth of the nuclear age, the public has demanded that governance criteria be served in vice presidential selection, lest electoral consequences be paid. Politicians, notably presidential nominees, have come to realize that good government and good politics are not that different when it comes to choosing vice presidents.

The lessons of this experience may be helpful in remedying the remaining flaws in the vice presidential selection process. The election criterion of uniting the party still can impede the selection of competent and loyal vice presidents. Any faction within a party that sets representation on the national ticket as the price for its support narrows the presidential nominee's range of choice severely and runs the risk of costing the party support in the general election. In addition, haste still can cloud judgment when vice presidential choices are being made, especially if the presidential nominating contest rages unresolved into the convention, distracting candidates until the last minute from the task of selecting a running mate.

The best lesson for dealing with these remaining problems, derived from experience, may be that changes in rules and procedures are less important than changes in electoral incentives. If the public continues to punish presidential nominees who choose inferior running mates, whatever the motive for choosing them, then future nominees will find other devices for uniting their parties than vice presidential nominations. If voters and journalists press candidates during the primary season to explain their thinking about the vice presidency and to describe their plans for choosing a running mate, candidates will give the matter more time and attention for fear of looking foolish or irresponsible.

### Unusual Selection

In discussions of each method of unusual vice presidential selection—the Twenty-fifth Amendment, Senate election, and national committee nomination—the main object of concern has been not so much electoral or even governance criteria as legitimacy. In all cases, the standby methods purport only to make the best of bad situations. On the rare occasions when these methods have been employed, the legitimacy of their use or result has not been seriously challenged.

As with the usual selection process, one can identify flaws, inherent or potential, in all the methods of unusual selection. But, again, as with the usual selection process, improvements are more likely to come about through public pressure than through changes in rules. Congressional confirmation hearings may take too long in some cases, but a dissatisfied public can prod legislators to expedite the process almost as effectively as a constitutional time limit, while allowing for a prolonged inquiry should circumstances require one. Representatives and senators may prefer that politically harmless nominations be made to fill a vacant presidency, but a president usually can force Congress's hand by rousing public opinion in favor of any competent nominee. The possibility of partisan shenanigans may inhere in the Senate election of the vice president that would follow an electoral college deadlock, but the risk of offending public notions of fairness is one that senators are bound to keep in mind. As for national parties, with the election still before them, they have every incentive to keep their proceedings free from any provocation to criticism.

# Chapter 4
# Activities

**W**idespread public concern about the vice presidency is mainly a product of the nuclear age. In a world shadowed by the possibility of virtually instant total war, Americans want the president's successor to be competent, loyal, and prepared. Changes in the vice presidential selection process have increased the likelihood that the first two of these standards will be met. The activities of vice presidents also have changed in recent years, mainly to assure the nation that a vice president will be ready, if called upon, to assume the presidency. It has become politically necessary for presidents to keep the vice president busy, informed, and in the public eye.

Modern presidents have other, perhaps more positive, incentives to make the vice president not just an active, but an influential member of the administration. The rapid growth of the national government and of the U.S. role in world affairs has increased the volume of demands from various groups and nations for presidential attention. The president can satisfy some of these demands by using the vice president as an emissary. Executive policymaking has become more centralized even as pressures have arisen to limit the size of the White House staff. The vice president, who also has a policy staff, is willing and usually able to help out the president. Decisionmaking in Congress has become steadily more fragmented. Again, the vice president and the legislative liaison staff are a ready resource. Finally, having probably chosen the vice president with governance criteria partly in mind, the president is likely to respect the vice president's abilities, trust the vice president's loyalty, and want to put the vice president to work in the administration.

That said, it also is true that the vice presidency is severely limited by its constitutional nature and, sometimes, by political constraints. Constitutionally, the vice presidency is a fundamentally weak office, with clear boundaries defining both the range of activities it can perform and the extent of influence in government it can achieve. No amount of change in the political environment or effort on the part of the president or vice president can alter that. Political constraints on vice presidential activity and influence, such as distrust by the White House staff, also exist but are more malleable.

Thus, even if the do-nothing vice presidency is a thing of the past, a do-nothing-important, or "Potemkin village," vice presidency still is possible. A vice president may be limited to titles, such as commission chair, and ceremonial duties (commencement speeches, goodwill trips abroad) that seem important but really are devoid of substance. "I go to funerals," lamented Vice President Nelson A. Rockefeller, describing his job toward the end of the term. "I go to earthquakes."[1]

## The Constitutional Vice Presidency

Some powers and duties of the vice presidency are grounded squarely in the Constitution. The vice president is president of the Senate, with the right to cast tiebreaking votes; holds a constitutionally independent office; has full successorship status in the event of a presidential vacancy; and is both the acting president during a period of presidential disability and the main figure in determining whether a president is disabled. Clearly, this is a weak array of formal powers. The irony is that what few responsibilities the Constitution does confer upon the vice presidency, for the most part, have weakened the office or retarded its development.

### President of the Senate

According to paragraph 4 of Article I, Section 3 of the Constitution, "The vice president of the United States shall be President of the Senate, but shall have no vote, unless they be equally divided." At one time, the vice president's Senate responsibilities were reasonably important. The first vice president, John Adams, operated in a manner not unlike a modern Senate majority leader, helping to shape the Senate's agenda and organizing and intervening in debate. He also decided, on average, nearly four tie votes each year during his two terms as vice president. In contrast, modern vice presidents have cast fewer than one tiebreaking vote every two years. (Even this small number exaggerates the importance of the power because, unless a measure is significant and the administration wants it to pass, the vice president's vote is of little consequence.) Similarly, modern vice presidents usually have treated their responsibility as Senate president in a passive and ceremonial way (one recent vice president spent only eighteen hours presiding over the Senate during an entire year), with deviations from that practice frankly frowned upon by senators. When Vice President Spiro T. Agnew wandered onto the Senate floor to ask Senator Len Jordan, a fellow Republican, if the administration could count on his vote for a tax bill, Jordan barked, "You had it until now," then vowed to oppose any bill that Agnew asked him to support. Rockefeller was severely criticized in the Senate for a controversial parliamentary ruling that he made concerning cloture, especially when he failed to recognize an opposing senator who wished to speak.[2]

What explains the atrophy of the vice president's constitutional power as president of the Senate? For one thing, the Senate has changed. As new states have been admitted, the number of senators has almost quadrupled from the original twenty-six, making tie votes statistically less probable. The Senate also has institutionalized, developing its own body of rules and procedural precedents, which the president of the Senate is expected merely to announce, on the advice of the parliamentarian. To be sure, until 1961 the vice president's only office was in the Capitol, and almost the entire vice presidential staff was funded by the congressional budget. But these were mere vestiges of the vice presidency's early legislative identity. In recent years the vice president's main offices have been in the west wing of the White House and in the Executive Office Building, with the bulk of the staff paid for by the executive budget.

A more important explanation for the decline in the vice president's Senate responsibilities is the ambiguous constitutional status of the office. A member of both (or neither) the executive and legislative branches, the vice presidency has never been fully at home in either one. In this century, to the extent that vice presidents have become closely identified with the presidents whose elections brought them to office, the Senate has become steadily less receptive to vice presidents who hope to play a formal role there. Nothing illustrates this better than the rebuff that Senate Democrats handed Lyndon B. Johnson, arguably the most effective Senate leader in history, when he asked to be allowed to continue presiding over meetings of the Senate Democratic conference at the start of his term as vice president in 1961. As Senator Clinton Anderson, one of Johnson's closest political allies, protested, the office of vice president simply is not a legislative office.[3]

*Independence*

The vice presidency is neither fully legislative nor fully executive. To be sure, a number of developments, notably the establishment by Franklin D. Roosevelt of the presidential nominee's right to designate a running mate, have moved the vice presidency more clearly into the executive orbit, in practice, if not in constitutional theory. The difference between theory and practice was decorously observed in the working relationship between President Dwight D. Eisenhower and Vice President Richard M. Nixon. Eisenhower firmly believed that the vice president "is not legally a member of the executive branch and is not subject to direction by the president." Thus, the president would never directly tell his vice president to do anything. Instead, recalls Nixon, Eisenhower would "wonder aloud if I might like to take over this or that project." Nixon, of course, never refused these requests. Indeed, he estimated after seven years as vice president that about 90 percent of his time had been spent on executive-branch activities, and only 10 percent on legislative matters. But, following constitutional form, Eisenhower said he regarded Nixon's efforts on the administration's behalf as "working voluntarily."[4]

In one very important sense, though, theory really does guide practice. The vice presidency, being an elective office with a fixed four-year term, is constitutionally independent. However closely the vice president may be associated with the administration, the president cannot command the vice president to do or not do anything, nor can the president fire the vice president.[5] In an extreme case, the president may even worry about alienating the vice president, for fear of making an enemy of a constitutional official who cannot be removed.

Aggravating the effects of vice presidential independence is the constitutional independence of the presidency. The first sentence of Article II—"The executive Power shall be vested in a President of the United States of America"—signifies that executive power is indivisible and lodges it in the presidency. The president can delegate such power to other officials in the executive branch, but only because they are not independent and thus can be held accountable. The president can remove executive officials and can "require the[ir] Opinion in writing."

The constitutional independence of the vice presidency, joined to the constitutional indivisibility of executive power, limits the range of responsibilities that the vice president can perform well in the executive branch. As Charles Kirbo, an adviser to President Jimmy Carter, observed, "You can't put the vice president in a position where the president will have to reverse him. If you put him in an executive function on a regular basis where you have got the risk of him doing something and then having the president go in there and turn it around, well, that is a bad relationship."[6] Indeed, virtually all attempts to give a vice president ongoing responsibility for an executive-branch activity have failed dismally. The range of failures, which includes assignments as diverse as agency head, staff director, commission chair, and, to some degree, member of the National Security Council (NSC), is so broad and diverse as to discourage presidents from making, and vice presidents from accepting, such assignments in the future.

*Executive assignments.* Henry A. Wallace, who served as vice president during Roosevelt's third term as president, was the first vice president to be made head of a government agency—and the last. In July 1941, Roosevelt named Wallace to chair the new Economic Defense Board, a three-thousand-member agency that was created by executive order and whose charge included imports, exports, stockpiling, shipping, international investments, and numerous other activities related to preparation for war. The responsibilities of the agency, which was renamed the Board of Economic Warfare shortly after Pearl Harbor, overlapped with those of several existing cabinet departments, notably State and Commerce. These overlaps generated severe and enervating interagency conflicts over jurisdiction and policy that weakened both the war effort and Wallace's authority. But because Roosevelt, for constitutional reasons, could not command or remove Wallace, at least not in the usual sense, he felt compelled to abolish the warfare board, which left the vice president embarrassed and devoid of function. What had seemed at the beginning to be a new day of vice presidential power turned out to be a false dawn. No subsequent president ever has asked the vice president to head an executive agency.

Rockefeller's experience as vice president offers a similar sad story. Rockefeller, who had long-standing expertise in domestic policy, won from President Gerald R. Ford permission to head the White House Domestic Council. The governor of New York at the time of his selection, Rockefeller took it as axiomatic that influence derives from position; as political mentor to Henry Kissinger, he thought he could be to domestic policy what Kissinger, as national security adviser to presidents Nixon and Ford, had been to foreign policy. But as vice president, constitutionally independent yet filling a staff position that otherwise would have been held by someone who served at the pleasure of the president, Rockefeller was perceived as a uniquely threatening figure by members of Ford's White House staff, especially chief of staff Donald Rumsfeld. Staff members slowed the flow of memoranda to and from Rockefeller, damned him with faint praise to the president and with harsh criticism in leaked stories to the press, disputed his domestic policy recommendations, and gave only grudging support to those recommendations that the president accepted. A few years later, the frustrated Rockefeller asked to be relieved of his Domestic Council responsibilities.

Even the relatively modest and familiar formal responsibilities that have been assigned to the vice presidency have foundered on the shoals of constitutional independence. Most modern vice presidents, beginning with Nixon, have been asked by the president to head various commissions, often on matters that the president, in response to interest-group or other public pressure, has wanted to deal with symbolically rather than substantively, such as youth employment, Native American opportunity, tourism, productivity and work quality, and intergovernmental relations. Unobjectionable as they may seem, vice presidential commissions usually fail, for reasons not unlike those that make it hard for a vice president's agency and staff assignments to succeed. Although commissions lack authority to make or implement policy, they often antagonize the parts of the executive branch that have regular jurisdiction over the areas being studied. As a result, vice presidents increasingly downplay commission work. Nixon does not even mention the commissions he chaired in his memoirs; Hubert H. Humphrey and Rockefeller headed numerous commissions but found the results to be so inconsequential that they later advised Vice President Walter F. Mondale to eschew commission work altogether. Agnew, chair of a commission that was supposed to untangle federal red tape for state and local governments, generally was ignored when mayors and governors discovered that he had no power to impose solutions. Ford and Mondale deliberately avoided commission assignments. "It's mostly a matter of listening to troubles," said a Ford aide, "which takes a lot of time without settling much of anything."[7]

The vice president's most impressive statutory responsibility, as member of the National Security Council, offers the final case of a formal executive assignment being subverted by constitutional independence. (The only other task assigned to the vice president by law is membership on the Board of Regents of the Smithsonian Institution.) Since the National Security Act was amended in 1949, the vice president has been one of the six officials serving on the NSC. As the only member whom the president cannot command or remove, the vice president is entitled to attend all NSC meetings for the entire term. It is a prestigious post, and for Nixon, the one vice president whose president relied heavily on the formal advisory structures of the executive branch, NSC membership really did provide an important channel of influence.

But few presidents want to feel obligated to involve the vice president in important foreign policy deliberations. As a result, they are likely either to call a limited number of NSC meetings or to use the meetings as forums to announce, rather than to make, policy. During the Cuban missile crisis, for example, President John F. Kennedy ignored the NSC, instead creating an ad hoc Executive Committee of the National Security Council to deal with the crisis. The "Excom" included all NSC members—except Vice President Johnson—and others, such as the attorney general and some White House aides. When he was president, Johnson did much the same: in his case, relying on an informal "Tuesday lunch" for Vietnam policymaking, including several NSC members but not Vice President Humphrey. When Humphrey raised doubts in the NSC about the administration's "Rolling Thunder" bombing campaign against North Vietnam in 1965, Johnson called no more meetings of the council for more than a year.

*Institutionalizing executive assignments.* Some vice presidents may feel compelled to accept an executive assignment in order to establish credibility within the administration. For example, during his first year in office, George Bush was still too much the outsider in the Reagan White House to pass up any opportunity to demonstrate his loyalty. In one case, to head off a major struggle that was developing among Richard Allen, the national security adviser; William Casey, the director of the Central Intelligence Agency; and Secretary of State Alexander Haig over responsibility in times of international crisis, the vice president was asked to head a newly formed Special Situations Group for crisis management. Bush agreed, which pleased the president and his aides, but shrewdly downplayed the assignment, placating Haig, Casey, and Allen. (It was nine months before the Special Situations Group held its first meeting.)

Political necessity is one thing; to go beyond that and propose that important executive assignments be made a regular feature of the vice presidency is another. Such proposals have been offered for many years. The argument usually runs along these lines: the president is overburdened, the vice president has little to do, so why not relieve the president of some responsibilities by giving them to the vice president? (Or: the vice presidency is the successor office, its lack of powers and duties discourages worthy political leaders from accepting it, so how can it be made more substantial and thus more appealing?) Clinton Rossiter suggested in 1948, for example, that the vice president "be designated in so many words as the president's chief assistant in the overall direction of the administrative branch," including responsibility for the development of the budget and the formulation of legislative proposals.[8] Rossiter later recanted, but the idea, or variations on it, lives on. In 1960, Nixon, then the Republican candidate for president, promised to use running mate Henry Cabot Lodge as a sort of first secretary of the government, coordinating the administration's foreign policy activities. At the 1980 Republican convention, aides to presidential nominee Ronald Reagan and former president Ford seriously discussed an arrangement in which Ford, as Reagan's vice president, would be the administration's equivalent of a corporate chief officer, with jurisdiction over the Office of Management and Budget and the National Security Council.

Proposals to assign formal authority to the vice president are inherently flawed for the simple reason that substantive executive powers cannot, in view of Article II, be delegated responsibly to any constitutionally independent official. Such proposals also suffer from the conflicts, suspicions, and resentments that the vice presidency's independence inevitably generates within the administration when executive assignments are made. As Mondale advised his successor, George Bush, "If such an assignment is important, it will then cut across the responsibilities of one or two cabinet officers or others and embroil you in a bureaucratic fight that would be disastrous. If it is meaningless or trivial, it will undermine your reputation and squander your time." Mondale further argued that, as vice president, "I don't have the staff to run a major line function. Nor should I. It takes a lot of time away from your advisory role."[9]

Finally, executive assignments may undermine the vice president's ability to fulfill the constitutional responsibility to succeed to the presidency in the event of a presidential vacancy. To prepare adequately to be president, the vice president needs broad and comprehensive experience in the administration. An executive assignment, particularly if it is important, will be time-consuming, limiting the vice president's attention to the range of tasks that the assignment entails. At a minimum, this will narrow the vice president's vision; at worst, it will lead to the familiar ill that plagues department and agency heads, namely, "capture" by a narrow slice of the executive bureaucracy. Also, should the expectation that the vice president will perform an executive assignment become institutionalized, it may warp the criteria for vice presidential selection.

The qualifications of a good agency head or staff director may be different from the qualifications of a worthy successor president.

*Constitutional status.* Some have suggested that the vice president be made a constitutional member of the executive branch.[10] As discussed earlier, in this century presidents and vice presidents have described the vice president[11] as everything from a dual member of Congress and the executive to a member of neither, the occupant of a constitutional "no-man's land." Why not amend the Constitution to remove the confusion and embody modern practice, the argument goes, and at the same time make the vice president a less alien figure within the executive branch?

But to amend the Constitution in this way would be mere bookkeeping. The main reason that vice presidents are unable to manage ongoing executive assignments successfully is not that they also serve as president of the Senate: that role has atrophied into inconsequence. Rather, the reason is that vice presidents are constitutionally independent—legally elected on their own for a fixed term and thus not subject to presidential command or removal.[12] Simply to declare in a constitutional amendment that the vice president is a member of the executive branch would not alter this status. And to the extent that the proposal is paired—as it often is—with a suggestion that the vice president be assigned ongoing responsibility as head of an important department, it ceases to be innocuous and instead falls prey to all the dangers that presently make executive assignments hazardous.[13]

### Successor

During most of its history, the vice presidency has been limited as an institution by its constitutional role as successor to the presidency. To borrow a distinction from classical physics, although the successor role gave the vice presidency great potential energy, it dampened the office's kinetic energy by fostering a certain tension in the relationship between president and vice president. Gouverneur Morris realized this at the Constitutional Convention. When Elbridge Gerry of Massachusetts (an opponent of the vice presidency who later became vice president) worried about the "close intimacy" that "must subsist between the president and vice president," Pennsylvania's Morris shrewdly replied, "The vice president will be the first heir apparent that ever loved his father."[14] More recently, Vice President Johnson expressed a similiar sentiment when he fretted that he felt like a "raven hovering around the president's neck."[15]

No doubt presidents still are sometimes reminded of their own mortality by the sight of the vice president. But, on the whole, the successor role has become a source of institutional strength for the vice presidency in recent years. Presidents in the postwar atomic age are expected by the public to recruit competent and loyal vice presidents and to prepare them to be president. Having recruited able people, of course, presidents also have become more likely to draw on their talents and expertise, thus making the vice presidency a more consequential office.

*Disability*

Sections 3 and 4 of the Twenty-fifth Amendment, as will be seen later, more than doubled the vice president's responsibilities during times of presidential disability. The original Constitution included a provision that the vice president would be acting president when the president was disabled, but rendered it meaningless by not creating a procedure to transfer power or to determine when a disability exists. The amendment not only created procedures, it made the vice president the central figure in identifying disabilities that the president was unable or unwilling to acknowledge.

For all their virtues, the disability provisions of the Twenty-fifth Amendment have been an albatross around the neck of the vice presidency. The shooting of President Reagan in 1981 presented the first real situation to arise under the Twenty-fifth Amendment. Constitutionally, after Reagan was anesthetized for surgery to remove the bullet, Vice President Bush's responsibility was to help decide whether a temporary transfer of power from the president to the vice president was warranted. Instead, fearing the wrath of the president or, more immediately, the White House staff, Bush stayed quietly on the sidelines.

Reagan's cancer operation in 1985 placed Bush in a different but equally precarious situation. This time, the president grudgingly invoked the Twenty-fifth Amendment and signed his powers and duties over to the vice president before his operation. (He reclaimed them eight hours later.) Bush stayed out of sight, relaxing quietly at the vice presidential residence. Inoffensive as the vice president's behavior was, it caused some tension between him and chief of staff Donald Regan, who would have preferred that Bush spend his time as acting president at his vacation home in Maine.

The Bush case suggests that, at best, the vice president's constitutional role under the Twenty-fifth Amendment has been enervated: the main figure in determinations of presidential disability is likely to be the White House staff, which, should a disability exist, typically will be inclined to restrict the vice president's activities as acting president.

Perversely, Bush strengthened his reputation in the Reagan White House by ceding control to the staff in the aftermath of the 1981 assassination attempt. The cancer operation in 1985 had the opposite effect. Indeed, the very existence of the vice president's constitutional powers in disability situations may have revived the old image—and the distrust that goes along with it—of a vice presidential "raven hovering around" the president's neck.

## Political Constraints

The constitutional nature of the vice presidency imposes sure and rather definite restrictions on the activities vice presidents can perform well. Political constraints on the vice presidency have been more variable— less powerful in the modern era than in the past, more of a problem for some vice presidents than for others. They also are more malleable. A careful, patient, politically shrewd vice president can overcome or at least minimize the political constraints on the office.

Two main political constraints can bind a vice president. First, the president may doubt the vice president's loyalty or competence. There may be personal tension between them: the vice president may have strenuously opposed, or even run against, the president in the past. Campaigns for presidential nominations often are fought by political leaders who share a basically similiar political philosophy, like Kennedy and Johnson or Reagan and Bush. But this only means that the contenders must exaggerate their policy disagreements and emphasize differences in their personal and professional qualifications, a strategy that sometimes manifests itself in heated, embittering rhetoric. Even if their differences are smoothed over in office, the president may wonder whether the vice president's future presidential ambitions (almost all vice presidents have had them) will cause their interests to diverge.

A president's doubts about a vice president's competence also may constrain a vice president's activities and influence. Some presidential running mates still are chosen according to a purely electoral criterion—to unite the party by appeasing a faction—that is unrelated to competence. Or the vice president may be talented and experienced, but not in ways that the president regards as useful to the administration. The managerial skills and knowledge of state politics that an able governor possesses, for example, are not readily transferable to a national office that is constitutionally unsuited for executive assignments. Thus, "outsider" vice presidents face greater obstacles than experienced Washington politi-

cians, especially if the president is an "insider." And even vice presidents
whose skills and expertise are of great value to an administration will lose
influence if, as the term wears on, their views become so predictable
that the president grows less interested in hearing them. "The president
can bestow assignments and authority and can remove that authority and
power at will," wrote former vice president Humphrey. "I used to call this
Humphrey's law—'He who giveth can taketh away and often does.'"[16]

The other main political constraint on the vice presidency is the White
House staff. The staff is a dangerous adversary, as vice presidents
Johnson, Humphrey, and Rockefeller learned to their regret. It can undermine, with a concerned word here and a smirk there, the president's
regard for the vice president's loyalty and competence and publicly em-
barrass the vice president with critical leaks to the press. It also can,
through delays and subterfuge, reduce the vice president's access to the
White House "paper flow," making timely and informed vice presidential involvement in important administration decisions more difficult.
As Paul Light has shown, each of the staff's two primary goals—to protect the president and to protect its own status as the main source of
presidential advice—generates jealousy and suspicion toward even the
president's appointees. When it comes to the vice president, matters
sometimes can reach a point at which, as an aide to Vice President
Rockefeller complained, "The president's men are always ready if the
president wants to cut the vice president out, but are deaf if the president wants him involved."[17]

Still, neither of the main political constraints on the vice presidency
is as likely to be felt, at least in severe form, in the modern era as in
the past. Presidential nominees, eager to be elected and to serve effectively in office, are more inclined than ever not only to apply the governance criteria of competence and loyalty to the selection of their running mates, but also to consider the talents and experience that the vice
president can bring to the administration. Outsider candidates, such as
Carter and Reagan, are especially likely to choose insider vice presidents,
a sensible form of ticket balancing and a way of acquiring a resource
that can be of genuine help in navigating unfamiliar Washington waters
after the election. For their part, vice presidents have learned that their
own political ambitions are inseparable from the president's success.
There is no political credit to be gained by undermining or distancing
oneself from the administration.

Outright hostility from the White House staff also is less probable
than in the past, although some degree of rivalry and suspicion seems

to be inevitable. Mondale and Bush worked hard to accommodate both of the staff's primary goals, laboring tirelessly in the president's service and with great deference to the staff; both did their best to seal the staff's goodwill by fostering working relationships between their own aides and the president's. Their examples offer future presidential advisers a way of looking at the vice president as an asset to themselves and the president rather than a threat.

In sum, political constraints are not as likely to hamper a vice president as in the past because presidents and their staffs are less likely to impose them. Traditional sources of tension have been muted. But there is another reason why the imposition of political constraints has become less draconian. In recent years, the vice presidency has evolved into a more formidable institution in its own right, one not easily relegated to obscurity. Its resources, notably staff, are considerable and would be hard to reduce to any great degree. Equally important, the extent and importance of the vice president's regular, and thus publicly expected, activities have expanded in ways that could not be easily reversed.

## The Institutional Vice Presidency

In his classic work, *The American Presidency,* Clinton Rossiter accurately described the modern presidency as less a succession of individual leaders than an institution, defined both by ongoing rules and expectations that shape its activities and by resources that enable it to function. In Rossiter's view, the most important institutional characteristic of the modern presidency is the congeries of roles it is expected to perform, which he called chief of state, chief of government, chief legislator, manager of prosperity, and voice of the people, among others. Rossiter was alert to the interrelatedness of the presidency's various roles, comparing the institution to a "stew whose unique flavor cannot be accounted for simply by making a list of ingredients." He also noted the importance of the institutional resources that allow a president to attempt to meet the office's full range of responsibilities: "Thousands at his bidding speed/ And post o'er land and ocean without rest."[18]

The vice presidency is not fully comparable to the presidency. Some of the president's most important roles, for example, are grounded in the Constitution, a document that limits more than it empowers the vice president. Certain presidential roles are formal and ongoing; as we have seen, the vice presidency is ill-suited to executive assignments. Nonetheless, much can be learned from a Rossiter-style analysis of the vice presidency as an institution. First, as discussed earlier, the vice presidency has developed enduring roles, including some mix of ceremonial activities; policy advice; public advocacy of the president's leadership, programs, and political party; legislative liaison; diplomatic travel; televised debates during the presidential campaign; and others. Second, the vice president's roles, like the president's, are interrelated: performance in one affects performance in others. Finally, the resources of the institutional vice presidency influence, and are influenced by, the roles it is called upon to fulfill. These resources now are considerable: offices in the Executive Office Building and the west wing of the White House, an executive budget, regular private meetings with the president, access to the White House paper flow, an official residence, and, most important, a staff that is large, specialized, and independently hired.

*Enduring Roles*

Most of the roles vice presidents now perform, like several of the presidential roles that Rossiter describes, were born of some combination of public expectations and presidential responses (and, sometimes, initiatives) that created precedents for the vice presidency as an institution. As we have seen, in the post-World War II era of cold war and atomic weaponry, the public came to expect presidents to select competent and loyal vice presidents and to prepare them for the possibility of succession. Presidents responded to these expectations by assigning new tasks to their vice presidents, which, when accepted by later presidents as precedents, became new institutional roles for the vice presidency. These new roles—some substantive, some symbolic, but almost all of them highly visible—have made the office more attractive to talented political leaders. And presidents, of their own volition and in their own interest, have been more willing to assign still further responsibilities to such leaders, ultimately creating additional roles for the vice presidency.

The Mondale vice presidency often is cited as the period in which all of these developments were manifested most fully. President Carter, recognizing both the widespread public concern about the vice presidency and the valuable uses to which a vice president could be put in an administration, selected Mondale with great care. Mondale, although a highly influential senator, jumped at the chance to run for vice president, aware of the new challenges of the office and the political and professional benefits of serving in it. When the term began, Carter not only allowed Mondale his choice of existing vice presidential roles, but took advantage of Mondale's Washington experience and personal competence by making him an intimate, wide-ranging general adviser.

The Mondale experience is atypical only in the degree of its success. Nine of the twelve vice presidents since 1932 have served in Congress, for example, which made them likely legislative liaisons, especially for the four presidents who had not. Rockefeller's long-standing knowledge of domestic policy made him an influential adviser to President Ford in that area, despite the other barriers to effectiveness he faced or, in some cases, created. Bush brought impressive foreign policy credentials to the Reagan administration. His experience as director of the Central Intelligence Agency, U.S. representative to the United Nations, and chief American diplomat in China made him a logical choice to undertake a variety of serious diplomatic assignments to China, the Soviet Union, and Western Europe during his first term as vice president.

### Interrelated Roles

The various roles of the vice presidency are interrelated in a number of ways. Performance in one role affects the vice president's capacity to perform some, or perhaps all, of the office's other roles. In most cases, success breeds success and failure breeds failure. Rockefeller, for example, cared much more deeply about his role as policy adviser than he did about publicly promoting and defending President Ford and the Republican party. By slighting the latter role, however, he engendered resentments among the White House staff that undercut his effectiveness as an adviser on matters of public policy. Bush, on the other hand, labored long and hard during the early part of his first term to perform the thankless tasks of the vice presidency, attending funerals and foreign inaugurations, chairing task forces and commissions, acting as liaison to black, Hispanic, and union leaders who were hostile to the policies of the Reagan administration, and campaigning tirelessly for Republican candidates around the country. After winning his spurs in the administration, Bush soon was entrusted with more substantial diplomatic and advisory responsibilities.

Occasionally, however, success in one role undermines the vice president's ability to fulfill others. Vice President Nixon was a highly effective party leader, regularly rousing Republican activists with slashing attacks on the Democratic party. Eisenhower, appreciating Nixon's enthusiasm but not his zeal, often was reluctant to entrust the vice president with diplomatic or advisory functions that required discretion or evenhandedness. More generally, as we will see, too effective a job as public advocate may reduce the vice president's capacity to be an effective successor to the presidency.

## *Roles and Resources*

The roles and the institutional resources of the vice presidency are linked in a synergistic way. Resources always have shaped roles. The vice president's office in the Capitol made participation in legislative liaisons sensible; the president's own liaison staff could use the office as a headquarters while involving the vice president in the ongoing process of congressional relations. The availability of free time enabled vice presidents to tour the country as public advocates for the president and the party. As one observer put it, "If you were [president and] fighting a war and had this weapon laying there, wouldn't you use it? That's what happened to vice presidents. As long as they were available, why not use them?"[19] New resources also have helped to make new roles possible. The vice president's ability to offer useful and intelligent advice to the president is greater than it used to be partly because the creation in 1969 of a vice presidential line item in the executive budget allowed vice presidents to hire talented staff people, and the granting of a west wing office put the vice president literally in the middle of the informal policy flow that surrounds the oval office.

New roles, in turn, are a source of new institutional resources. In late 1976, during the transition period, Mondale convinced President-elect Carter that the vice president should work mainly as a general adviser and troubleshooter for the president. He then argued that to perform these roles adequately, he would need a broad array of resources, including full access to all the information the president received, the right to require other executive officials to meet his requests for information, a large, capable, and independently hired staff, a working relationship with the president's staff, permission to see the president whenever necessary, and freedom from ongoing executive assignments. Carter, persuaded that the roles he wanted Mondale to perform required such resources, approved the vice president's requests in full and added a west wing office.[20]

## Conclusion

Taken together, the main elements of the institutional vice presidency—the development of new and significant roles, the interrelatedness of these roles, and the mutual effects of roles and resources—have made the office both more attractive to political leaders and more active and influential in the councils of the American presidency. The curious constitutional nature of the vice presidency ordains that its more substantial roles will never derive from legal doctrine. But, as Rossiter showed in discussing the presidency, roles can be as solidly grounded in public expectations and presidential precedents as in formal decrees. In the case of the vice presidency, the ideal role, both for the president and the vice president, is that of general adviser. As Mondale argued in his pre-inaugural memo to Carter, this is the role that, as a nationally elected politician (presidents have few such politicians around them in the White House) who is unburdened by ongoing responsibilities (presidents also have few unburdened aides to draw on), the vice president is best equipped to perform. It also is the role that, by allowing the vice president to range widely, offers the best preparation for succession.

Just as laws and the Constitution are not a source of vice presidential influence, the problems that beset the institutional vice presidency are unlikely to be solved by new laws or constitutional amendments. These problems have mainly to do with the vice president's activities as public advocate. Advocacy is what earns some vice presidents the trust within the White House that they need to exercise the office's more substantial roles—policy aide, diplomat, and especially, general adviser. Advocacy, which will be explored in the next chapter, can also enhance the vice president's standing in the party and thus set the stage for a successful presidential nomination campaign. But overly enthusiastic advocacy of the president's leadership, programs, and party is likely to have three bad side effects on the vice president. It can make the vice president a divisive figure in national politics; it can place vice presidents on record as endorsing administration positions they personally do not agree with; and it can make vice presidents appear parrotlike and thus weak. In different ways, each of these side effects of the public advocacy role undermines the vice president's ability to serve as a strong and unifying successor if the presidency should become vacant.

This dilemma—namely, that vice presidents may pay too high a price for the influence within the administration that they seek[21]—has led the political scientist Joseph Pika to suggest that a vice president may do better to stay "out of the loop and above the fray"—that is, to sacrifice some of the benefits of being an administration insider for the sake of a certain measure of independence.[22] In certain cases, this is an appealing stance—in hindsight, Bush certainly would have preferred to have been completely outside the loop of the Reagan administration's arms-for-hostages policymaking process. But as a general course, Pika's recommendation is extreme, and not one that most vice presidents are likely to follow anyway, for fear of alienating the president, the White House staff, and the president's supporters, whose animus could be fatal if the vice president ever sought the party's nomination for president. The real challenge for the vice president is to maintain a delicate balance between loyal advocacy and abject servility. Mondale may have offered fellow vice presidents the best advice (all the better because he followed it himself) in a memo to his successor:

> As a spokesman for the Administration, stay on the facts. A president does not want and the public does not respect a vice-president who does nothing but deliver fulsome praise of a president. . . .[23]

# Chapter 5
# Succession and Disability

$\mathbf{M}$ ore than anything else, what makes discussions of vice presidential selection and of vice presidential activities important is the possibility that the vice president one day will wield the authority of the president. Constitutionally, the vice president succeeds to the presidency upon the death, resignation, or impeachment and removal of the president. In the event of a presidential disability, the vice president serves as acting president.[1] And, of course, a vice president may become president by being elected to office.

## Succession

Vice presidential succession is the subject of a substantial chapter in the history of the American presidency. Nine successor vice presidents have served twenty-six years as president. Counting the time they spent in the office after winning terms in their own right, successor vice presidents have been president for forty-two years, twenty-nine of them in this century. During one recent period from 1945 to 1977, vice presidents who became president by succession occupied the Oval Office almost half the time. Illnesses, impeachment proceedings, and assassination attempts have made succession an active possibility during twenty of the nation's forty presidencies.[2] Every postwar vice president except Walter F. Mondale has become the subject of unusual public concern because of some event that raised the possibility that he would succeed to the presidency.

The United States is unique among the major nations of the world in having an official whose main function is to be, if and when necessary, successor to the leader of the government and who, upon succession, serves out the unexpired balance of the leader's term. Both of these characteristics of the vice president's successor role evolved through history; neither was intended by the framers of the Constitution. Although presidential succession was a concern of the Constitutional Convention, the delegates' primary purpose in creating the vice presidency was to make the electoral college work. What is more, they almost certainly intended that succession to the presidency would be temporary, pending a special presidential election.[3]

The framers' intentions regarding succession and a special election were obscured because of what can only be called clerical error. The Committee of Style, created at the end of the convention to put the delegates' myriad decisions into a final draft of the Constitution, was given two succession resolutions to incorporate, one from a report by the Committee of Eleven that was submitted to the convention on September 4, the other from a motion that was made on the floor by Edmund Randolph of Virginia and approved on September 7. The first resolution stated: "In case of his [the president's] removal as aforesaid, death, absence, resignation, or inability to discharge the powers or duties of his office the Vice President shall exercise those powers and duties until another President be chosen, or until the inability of the President be removed." The second resolution, which was intended to supplement the first by providing a method for presidential succession if there were no vice president, read: "The Legislature may declare by law what officer of the United States shall act as President in the case of death, resignation, or disability of the President and Vice President; and such Officer shall act accordingly, until such disability be removed, or a President shall be elected." The last nine words of the latter resolution were James Madison's amendment to Randolph's motion, and were inserted expressly to permit "a supply of vacancy by an intermediate election of the President."[4]

What appeared in the final draft by the Committee of Style, which was mildly modified by the convention, was the product of the committee's effort to compress the two resolutions into one, now paragraph 6 of Article II, Section 2:

> In case of the Removal of the President from the Office, or of his Death, Resignation, or Inability to discharge the Powers and Duties of the said Office, the Same shall devolve on the Vice President, and the Congress may by law provide for the Case of Removal, Death, Resignation, or Inability,

both of the President and Vice President, declaring what Officer shall then act as President, and such officer shall act accordingly, until the Disability be removed, or a President shall be elected.

Clearly, the framers' intentions regarding succession were obscured, no doubt unwittingly, by the committee. Grammatically, it is impossible to tell—and in their rush to adjournment the delegates did not notice the ambiguity—whether "the Same" in the provision refers to "the said Office" (the presidency) or, as the convention intended, to its "Powers and Duties"; nor can one ascertain if "until . . . a President shall be elected" means until the end of the original four-year term or, again, as intended, until a special election is held. Because the official and unofficial records of the convention were kept secret for many years, no one could consult the debates to clear up the confusion. And because the new republic went fifty-two years without experiencing a vacancy in the presidency—more than double the length of any later period of uninterrupted presidential service—there were no surviving delegates from the convention to clear matters up when President William Henry Harrison died shortly after his inauguration in 1841.

Initially, Harrison's cabinet and some others seemed to think that the president's death made Vice President John Tyler only the acting president. Tyler believed differently—he quickly took the oath of office as president, delivered a sort of inaugural address, declared his intention to serve out the remainder of Harrison's term, and moved into the White House. Tyler's decisiveness prevailed in a constitutionally and politically uncertain situation. An effort in Congress to address him in correspondence as "Vice President, on whom, by the death of the late President, the powers and duties of the offices of President have devolved" failed miserably.[5]

Tyler's full, if constitutionally dubious, succession established a lasting precedent. Not only did future vice presidents succeed to the presidency without a second thought about the propriety of the action, their right to the office was accepted without controversy. For all the nonsense of the so-called Tecumseh's curse, familiar to every schoolchild, which holds that every president elected in a year ending with zero will die in office, it serves as mnemonic for the continuing frequency of presidential successions: Andrew Johnson, after Abraham Lincoln died in 1865; Chester A. Arthur, who succeeded James Garfield in 1881; Theodore Roosevelt, after William McKinley's death in 1901; Calvin Coolidge, the successor to Warren G. Harding in 1923; Harry S. Truman, after Franklin D. Roosevelt in 1944; and Lyndon B. Johnson, who succeeded John F. Kennedy in 1963. (Evidently Zachary Taylor's death in 1850 and Richard M. Nixon's resignation in 1974, with vice presidents Millard Fillmore and Gerald R. Ford, respectively, succeeding them, happened independently of the curse.)

Despite this accumulation of precedents, the Constitution until recently remained vague about succession, even though several amendments touched on the subject. The Twelfth Amendment seemed to suggest, albeit offhandedly and not by clear congressional intent, that the vice president was to be acting president.[6] In providing for a failure of both the electoral college and the House of Representatives to elect a president by the start of the term, the Twelfth Amendment said that "the Vice President shall act as President, as in the case of the death or other constitutional disability of the President." The provision later was replaced by the Twentieth Amendment, which said more blandly that, if a president had not been elected by inauguration day, "the Vice President shall act as President until a President shall have qualified." The Twenty-second Amendment left the matter explicitly unresolved, stating that "no person who has held the office of President, or acted as President for more than two years of a term to which some other person was elected President shall be elected to the office of the President more than once." Not until 1967 was the Constitution brought into conformity with more than a century of practice. Section 1 of the Twenty-fifth Amendment dealt directly with this issue: "In case of the removal of the President from office or of his death or resignation, the Vice President shall become President."

### Succession by Special Election?

The traditional (and now constitutional) succession process has many critics, most of whom regard it as inadequate to the task of assuring the nation effective leadership and would prefer that vacancies in the presidency be filled by special election. Vice presidents are not likely to be of presidential caliber, proponents of a special election argue. They are chosen according to election, not governance, criteria. (Or, as former representative James O'Hara put it, presidential candidates will not choose running mates "to succeed them. They will choose them to succeed.") Nor is the experience of being vice president helpful preparation for the presidency. According to Eric Goldman, the historian and former aide to President Johnson, "If a man of ability and spirit is chosen [to be vice president], he is being placed in a role that is certain to be miserable, likely to be demeaning, and may well—depending on the personalities and circumstances—seriously corrode his potential for effective leadership in the future."[7]

Critics of vice presidential succession are as convinced of the virtues of a special election as of the weaknesses of the vice presidency. One line of advocacy is avowedly idealistic: American practice should conform to the original constitutional intent that the president "be elected," an ideal later enshrined, at least in part, in the 1792 and 1886 succession acts, which provided for a special election in the event of a double vacancy in the presidency and vice presidency.[8] The other main argument for a special election, practical in nature, draws attention to the experience of the French Fifth Republic. The constitution of France, which also provides for a presidential system, states that, in the event of a vacancy in the presidency, the president of the Senate shall serve as the government's caretaker until a special election is held within five weeks to choose a new president for the full term of office. In 1974, when President Georges Pompidou died, the special election took place thirty-three days afterward, followed by a runoff two weeks later, and the inauguration of a new president eight days after that.

In the most advanced version of the special election proposal, Arthur M. Schlesinger, Jr., suggests some American variations on the French practice. Because any designated caretaker from Congress could well be a leader of a party different from the late president's, the acting president should be a member of the administration, preferably the secretary of state. Because American political parties are large and diffuse, the special election should not take place until ninety days after the vacancy, with the parties' national committees choosing candidates. Finally, to allow the usual presidential selection process to run its course, no special election should be held if a vacancy occurs during the final year of a president's tenure. Instead, the caretaker should serve out the term.[9]

What of the vice presidency in this new scheme? Logically, the office need not be abolished in the course of instituting special elections. Vice presidents still would have constitutional duties as the Senate president and would be the vital figure in situations of presidential disability, in addition to performing certain of their ongoing modern activities and, perhaps, a new responsibility as caretaker pending the special election. But, as Schlesinger realizes, the office would best be eliminated under the special election proposal. It would be difficult to attract competent people to the vice presidency if it were stripped of its successor role, in which case even the office's limited powers would be exercised poorly.

Also, after a special election brought in a new president, the vice presidency might well be occupied by a member of the opposition party, a problem best headed off by abolition.

Appealing as the special election idea may be, it has attracted a variety of critics. Some identify problems in the proposal itself. Unlike France, the United States is a superpower; it cannot afford the uncertainty that would attend caretaker leadership, especially in view of the frequency with which presidential vacancies have occurred. Also, unlike France, presidential selection in the United States is an inherently lengthy undertaking: the nominating process is diffuse, the pool from which presidents are drawn is broad, and time is required for voters and political activists to sort through all the alternatives. Staffing a new president's administration and developing its policies also are time-consuming. In practice, the proposed ninety-day interregnum, itself long, might effectively last thirty to sixty days longer, with the added time serving as a de facto transition period for the new president.

Other criticisms of the special election proposal concern its actual operation. For example, would the caretaker president be allowed to run in the special election? If not, the nation would be guaranteed a lack of continuity in leadership and, perhaps, deprived of an able president. If so, how would the caretaker's candidacy influence the conduct of the temporary "administration"? And how would the selection of people to fill the office that provides the caretaker be affected? The qualifications of a good acting president and those of, say, a good secretary of state may be different. Other questions come to mind. Could the parties' national committees do an adequate job of nominating the presidential candidates, an assignment for which they have little experience? Would the presidential and congressional elections remain forever unsynchronized? Would the caretaker be granted the full range of presidential powers and duties?

In addition to attacking the special election idea, some have defended the virtues of vice presidential succession. Above all, they argue, the traditional procedure of instant, certain, and full succession by the vice president is a source of stability in the political system. Presidential deaths are, in a literal sense, traumatic events for many citizens, triggering feelings not only of personal grief but of fear for the republic.[10] In this uncertain and emotional setting, Americans historically have accepted the vice president's succession as legitimate; indeed, survey data for the past three successions show the public rallying to each new president's support to an extent unrivaled by even the most popular elected president.[11]

Legitimacy and stability are qualities of the historic system of vice presidential succession; they are not qualities that a polity can take for granted when there are leadership changes.

Beyond the virtues of vice presidential succession as a procedure in its own right, one can argue that the system also works well in practice, by providing able presidents when needed. In the view of historians, the five twentieth-century successor presidents actually rate slightly higher, as a group, than the century's ten elected presidents.[12] Voters have agreed, electing four of the five successors to full terms while rejecting the reelection bids of three of the ten originally elected presidents. And, as was evident in the two preceding chapters, changing electoral incentives mean that vice presidents in the late twentieth century are chosen more with their successor role in mind, and are better prepared for it while in office, than at any time in history. In a real sense, proponents of a special election are prescribing a cure for an ailment that is healing of its own accord.

### Pre-inaugural Succession

The certainty that is such a virtue of the presidential succession process does not characterize current provisions for pre-inaugural succession. Section 3 of the Twentieth Amendment deals with the matter in part: it provides that the vice-president-elect is to become president if the president-elect dies. But "elect" status only exists during the two-week period between January 6, when Congress counts the electoral votes for president and vice president and declares the winners, and January 20, when the new term begins. Succession procedures for the period from the national nominating conventions, six to seven months prior to the inauguration, to January 6 are less well defined.

If a presidential nominee died or left the ticket between the convention in July or August and election day in November, the national party probably would choose the vice presidential nominee as the replacement; that choice would be even more likely if a vacancy on the winning presidential ticket occurred between election day and the day in mid-December when the electors cast their ballots, considering that the vice presidential nominee would by then have received a national endorsement of sorts. But such a decision by the party is not guaranteed, which has prompted one scholar to propose that Congress enact legislation covering this possibility.[13]

The death of a presidential candidate between mid-December and January 6 would pose the most difficult situation of all. Because Congress has failed to legislate for this possibility, as it is called upon to do in Section 4 of the Twentieth Amendment, it would be left with the absurd task of choosing between the dead winning candidate, prompting an immediate vice presidential succession to the presidency on inauguration day, and the nominee of the losing party.

## Disability

Article II, Section 1, paragraph 6 of the original Constitution, which was imprecise about presidential succession, was triply so on the subject of disability. The meanings of death, resignation, and impeachment—the events that prompt a succession—are clear. A procedure, if not useful criteria, for impeachment is spelled out in the Constitution; death and resignation, obviously, present only minor procedural issues. But the language of the Constitution pertaining to disability initially was so vague as to be meaningless: "In the case of . . . Inability [of the president] to discharge the Powers and Duties of the said Office, the Same shall devolve on the Vice President . . . until the Disability be removed, or a President shall be elected." "What is the extent of the term 'disability,'" John Dickinson of Pennsylvania asked the Convention on August 20, "and who is to be the judge of it?" No one answered him.[14]

Lack of a definition for disability or a procedure for temporarily removing a disabled president left the nation without a leader for parts of at least eleven presidencies prior to 1967. Garfield, who hovered near death for eighty days after he was shot (fatally, as it turned out) in 1881, and Woodrow Wilson, an apparent invalid for the final seventeen months of his second term, offer the most notorious examples. In Garfield's case, the cabinet, including the attorney general, believed that, in view of Tyler's interpretation of paragraph 6, presidential power could only be transferred to the vice president permanently; there would be no getting it back if the president were to recover. Wilson's cabinet and many members of Congress were more disposed to transfer power to Vice President Thomas R. Marshall, but the Constitution's lack of guidance and a protective White House staff stayed their hands. When Secretary of State Robert Lansing broached the subject with Joseph Tumulty, Wilson's secretary, Tumulty replied, "You may rest assured that while Woodrow Wilson is lying in the White House on the broad of his back I will not be a party to ousting him." Marshall confided to his secretary, "I am not going to seize the place and then have Wilson—recovered—come around and say 'get off, you usurper.'"[15]

President Dwight D. Eisenhower's ailments—a heart attack in 1955, an ileitis attack and operation in 1956, and a stroke in 1957—finally brought matters to a head. In an age of nuclear confrontation, he and many others felt, the nation could not run the risk of being leaderless even for an hour. Eisenhower's short-term solution was to write Vice President Richard M. Nixon a letter stating that, if the president ever were disabled again, he would instruct the vice president to serve as acting president until the disability passed. If Eisenhower were unable to communicate for some reason, Nixon could make the decision himself. In either event, Eisenhower would decide when it was time for him to resume the powers and duties of the presidency.

Presidents Kennedy and Johnson endorsed this arrangement when they took office, but it hardly solved the problem. For one thing, a letter, even a presidential letter, lacks the force of law. The legality of any veto, appointment, military order, or other action taken by a vice president acting as president under such authority could be challenged at the time or afterward. Equally important, the Eisenhower arrangement made no provision to relieve a president who was disabled but, like Wilson, refused to admit it. To deal with these problems, Congress included a disability procedure when it passed the Twenty-fifth Amendment in 1965.

Three very different situations are provided for by the disability provisions of the Twenty-fifth Amendment. In the first, covered in Section 3, the president is temporarily "unable to discharge the powers and duties of his office" and recognizes it. Such a situation could arise if the president's doctors advised complete rest while recovering from a stroke or similar malady, or if the president were going to be anesthetized during an operation. (It was just such an event that prompted Eisenhower to lament, after he had been in surgery for two hours, that "the country was without a Chief Executive, the armed forces without a Commander-in-Chief.")[16] In either case, the president would sign a letter to the president pro tempore of the Senate and the Speaker of the House announcing disability. The vice president then would become acting president. When able, the president would write a letter to the congressional leaders and, within four days, resume office.

The second situation, which is anticipated in Section 4, is one in which the president is disabled but unable to say so, perhaps because of loss of consciousness. In this case, the vice president or the head of an executive department could call a cabinet meeting to discuss the situation. The vice president clearly is the central figure in this process; Section 4 authorizes Congress, by a simple majority vote, to replace the cabinet with some other group in disability determinations, but not the vice president. If the vice president and a majority of the department heads (or the congressionally designated group) agreed that the president was disabled, the vice president would become acting president. When able, the president would write a letter to the congressional leaders and, within four days, resume office.

The Twenty-fifth Amendment's provisions for the first two situations essentially codified the main points of the Eisenhower letter. But what would happen if a disability were in doubt, if the vice president and cabinet said that the president was disabled and the president claimed to be able? In many such instances (suspected mental illness, physical paralysis, sudden loss of sight or hearing), there would be room for honest disagreement about whether a severe disability existed. The Twenty-fifth Amendment deliberately gives no definition to the word "inability." It is clear from the congressional debates that inability is not unpopularity, incompetence, laziness, or impeachable conduct. As to what inability is, Congress thought it best to leave the term undefined so that those actually confronted with the need to make such a determination would not be bound by an outdated or incomplete definition.[17] Thus, any decision regarding presidential disability would be by its nature subjective.

If the vice president and a majority of the cabinet were to declare the president disabled and the president disagreed, Section 4 provides that Congress would decide who it thought was right, taking no longer than three weeks to do so. (In the meantime, the vice president would be acting president.) If, within that three-week period, two-thirds of the House and Senate, voting separately, decided against the president, the vice president would continue to serve as acting president. If one-third plus one of either house sided with the president, the vice president would turn back the powers and duties of the office.

But even a vote by Congress would not necessarily be the end of it. For after Congress made an adverse judgment, the president could, in a day or a week or whenever, start the whole process over by claiming to be able once again. As many times as the president did so, Congress would have to decide the issue. The prospect of such a president rousing public sympathy could discourage the vice president and the cabinet from acting in the first place.

Similarly, if one-third plus one of either house of Congress sided with the president, there would be nothing to stop the vice president and cabinet from again declaring the president disabled and throwing the issue back to Congress for another vote. The president could fire all the department heads and try to replace them with supporters—Truman once said that if his cabinet removed him while he was flat on his back his first act upon rising would be to send them all packing.[18] But, of course, Congress then could replace, by simple majority vote, the cabinet with some other group, perhaps one of its committees. If this new body should agree with the vice president that the president was disabled, the issue would go back to Congress again.

None of the more dramatic incidents that one could imagine arising under the disability provisions of the Twenty-fifth Amendment has yet occurred. What is distressing, though, is that the amendment failed its first real test and barely passed its second, even though the situations seemed straightforward. When Ronald Reagan was shot on March 30, 1981, it was clear to all that he would be anesthetized for surgery for an indefinite period. International tensions were high. It seemed all too possible that Soviet troops might enter Poland at any time. Yet presidential aides at the hospital privately decided not to ask Reagan to sign over his powers to Vice President George Bush under Section 3. Soon after, aides at the White House, where members of the cabinet had assembled, headed off any discussion of invoking Section 4. Four days later, when Reagan ran a sudden high fever, requiring more sedation so that a bronchoscopy could be performed, aides again explicitly decided that there would be no cabinet discussion of constitutional disability. Their motive in all cases seems to have been to forestall public confusion, particularly any suggestion that the president was not in control.[19]

The first result of the decision not to invoke the Twenty-fifth Amendment was that once again "the country was without a Chief Executive, the armed forces without a Commander-in-Chief." The second was widespread anxiety about who really was in charge while Reagan was unconscious. Shortly after the shooting, Secretary of State Alexander Haig rushed before television cameras to say that he was "in control," at least until Bush returned to Washington. But, constitutionally, neither Haig, Bush, nor anyone else could have exercised the powers of the presidency during the critical hours of surgery and recuperation.

Criticism of the administration's failure to act in 1981 shaped its preparation for Reagan's cancer surgery on July 13, 1985. This time the president sent letters to the House speaker and the Senate president both before and after the surgery—the first relinquishing his powers and duties to Bush, the second reclaiming them. Strangely, however, Reagan did not explicitly invoke Section 3 of the Twenty-fifth Amendment in his letters, instead writing that he was not convinced that the amendment was meant to apply to "such brief and temporary periods of incapacity" as his surgery. As for Bush, he spent his eight hours as acting president quietly at home, chatting with friends and playing tennis.

### Concerns about Disability

One early fear about the disability provisions of the Twenty-fifth Amendment, forcefully articulated by Congressman Henry B. Gonzalez of Texas, was that Section 4 was a "standing invitation" to the vice president and cabinet "to overthrow the President."[20] In truth, this fear never was well founded—even if a president's colleagues seized the powers of the office, a farfetched possibility, they still would have to convince two-thirds of the House and Senate to approve their coup. A more reasonable criticism of the amendment, in view of recent experience, is that it assumes too much willingness on the part of the vice president and cabinet to step forward and act in an uncertain and politically precarious situation. In practice, when questions of disability arise, it is the White House staff, not the constitutionally designated officials, that is most likely to determine what happens.

A second early fear about the disability amendment, as yet unrefuted by experience, involves the lack of terminus in Section 4. Because the transfer of powers and duties from president to vice president is meant to cover only the period of disability, the president is always entitled to reclaim them, even if it seems to others that the disability persists. The prospect of a half-crazed Lear stalking Washington and the nation, howling for vindication and tying up the government until the four-year term expires, is not entirely fanciful. More dangerous, perhaps, would be the president whose mental disability, although known to those in government, could be disguised in carefully managed public appearances.

A more recent concern aroused by the Twenty-fifth Amendment involves the physical and mental abilities of the vice president. The disability provisions assume that the vice president will be entirely able during any period of presidential disability. The vice presidential selection provision, by assuring that a vice president almost always will be available to succeed to the presidency in the event of a death, impeachment, or resignation, also takes for granted that the vice president will be able. This assumption, of course, is by no means warranted. Yet neither the Twenty-fifth Amendment nor any other part of the Constitution provides for vice presidential disability.

Finally, presidents and their staff assistants have attached a stigma of presidential weakness and public confusion to temporary disability that the authors of the Twenty-fifth Amendment had hoped would not exist. Reagan's transfer of power to Bush in 1985 may have helped to mitigate this condition; future presidents who undergo surgery probably will regard it as a precedent. But perhaps not: Reagan's letter to Congress was grudging in tone, hazy about its grounding in the Twenty-fifth Amendment, and explicit in stating that the president was "not intending to set a precedent binding anyone privileged to hold this office in the future." In all likelihood, brief transfers of power would be understood for what they are by the public and by other nations and regarded as acts of presidential responsibility. But unless presidents invoke the amendment routinely, the onus attached to its use will become real.

## Electoral Succession

In addition to the succession and disability paths to the White House, the vice president also can become president by being elected to the office. Indeed, one of the most extraordinary qualities of the modern vice presidency is that it now is typically taken for granted that the vice president will run for president and lead the field in the race for the party's nomination.

The role of the vice presidency as springboard to the presidency is an entirely new one in this century—no nineteenth-century vice president after Martin Van Buren was seriously considered for a presidential nomination, not even the four vice presidents who succeeded to the presidency. Theodore Roosevelt's vice presidency marks one turning point in this regard: he was nominated for president in 1904 after succeeding to the office when McKinley died, setting the pattern for all future successor vice presidents. Roosevelt also was the first of fifteen twentieth-century vice presidents (out of nineteen) later to seek the presidency. Of the exceptions, death or ill health account for three—James S. Sherman, Charles Curtis, and Nelson A. Rockefeller—and criminal conviction the fourth, Spiro T. Agnew.[21]

In the 1950s, the Nixon vice presidency opened an even more significant chapter in the electoral history of the vice presidency. Starting with Nixon, every vice president has led in a majority of the Gallup surveys that measure voters' preferences for their party's presidential nomination.[22] In all three of the elections since 1960 in which the president did not or could not run for reelection, the incumbent party has nominated the vice president as its presidential candidate. Six of the eight most recent vice presidents, again beginning with Nixon, have been nominated for president: Nixon, Johnson, Humphrey, Ford, Mondale, and Bush. Even a vice presidential nomination is now a springboard of sorts: five of the seven losing vice presidential candidates since 1960—Henry Cabot Lodge, Edmund Muskie, Sargent Shriver, Robert A. Dole, and Mondale—later showed support in presidential nominating contests.

What is the explanation for this recent ascendancy of the vice presidency as an electoral office? Theodore Roosevelt and his successors took advantage of new national media and new norms of campaigning to make the vice president a more widely known and politically better established figure. Nixon and later vice presidents capitalized on three other important developments. First, the two-term limit that was imposed on presidents by the Twenty-second Amendment, ratified in 1951, made it possible for the vice president to launch a presidential campaign during the president's second term without unduly alienating the president. (This effect of the amendment, which was wholly unanticipated, may be almost as great as its intended effect on the presidency.) Second, the role Nixon developed, with Eisenhower's encouragement, as party builder—campaigning during elections, raising funds in between them— and public advocate of the administration and its policies uniquely situates the vice president to win friends among the political activists who influence presidential nominations. Such campaigning also is good training for a national presidential campaign. Finally, the recent growth in the governmental roles and resources of the vice presidency has made it a more prestigious position, and consequently a more plausible stepping-stone to the presidency. Foreign travel and the trappings of the office—the airplane, mansion, seal, west wing office, and so on—are physical symbols of prestige.[23] Perhaps more important, in their efforts to assure the nation that they are fulfilling their responsibility to prepare for a possible emergency succession, presidents tend to make inflated claims about the role of the vice president in the administration. Thus, the typical modern vice president can plausibly argue, as Mondale frequently did, that the vice presidency "may be the best training of all" for the presidency:

> I'm privy to all the same secret information as the president. I have unlimited access to the president. I'm usually with him when all the central decisions are being made. I've been through several of those crises that a president

invariably confronts, and I see how they work. I've been through the budget process. I've been through the diplomatic ventures. I've been through a host of congressional fights as seen from the presidential perspective.[24]

Yet, for all their electoral advantages, vice presidents who have won the nominations of their parties for president typically have lost in the general election: no incumbent vice president has been elected to the presidency since 1836. This is not to say that vice presidents are destined to lose—Nixon in 1960 and Humphrey in 1968 barely were defeated, and Bush may well be a strong candidate in 1988. But vice presidents carry certain burdens into the fall campaign that are as surely grounded in their office as the advantages they had brought to the earlier contest for the nomination.

In fact, some of the activities of the modern vice presidency that are most appealing to the party activists who influence nominations may repel many members of the broader electorate that decides the election. Days and nights spent fertilizing the party's grass roots with fervent, sometimes slashing, rhetoric can alienate voters, who look to the presidency for unifying, not partisan, leadership. So can the vice president's role as advocate of the president's policies. Some administrations have relied on the vice president to defend their least popular actions and programs, freeing the president to dwell on more universally appealing proposals and accomplishments. (That was the fate of Vice President Humphrey on the Vietnam issue.) Such a course is likely to win the vice president friendship and influence in the west wing, but may lead voters to associate the vice president with controversy.

Certain institutional qualities of the modern vice presidency, some of which have helped raise the office to its recent stepping-stone status, also handicap the vice-president-turned-presidential-candidate. The vice president cannot plausibly claim credit for the successes of the administration—that is a presidential prerogative. But the vice president can be attacked by the other party's presidential candidate for the administration's shortcomings. Such attacks allow no good response. A vice president who tries to stand apart from the administration will alienate the president and cause voters to wonder why the criticisms were not voiced earlier, when they might have made a difference. The vice president can say instead that loyalty to the president forecloses public disagreement, but that course is no less perilous. Strength, independence, vision, and integrity are the qualities voters seek most in a president, not loyalty.

*Discussion*

The modern vice presidency is uniquely blessed and uniquely cursed in electoral politics. The new activities of the office make it the clearest path to a nomination for president, which in turn makes it attractive to a wider range of presidential-caliber politicians. Yet the self-effacing, intensely loyal behavior that vice presidents must engage in if they are to partake of the office's political benefits in a nominating contest is a handicap in a general election.

No doubt most vice presidents understand the electoral tensions that inhere in the office, which were well stated by President Eisenhower: "To promise and pledge *new* effort, *new* programs, and *new* ideas without appearing to criticize the current party and administration—that is indeed an exercise in tightrope walking."[25] But they also realize that presidential nominations are hard to come by and that, for all but a few political luminaries, the vice presidency represents their best chance to win one. And they remember that Eisenhower's vice president, Nixon, almost crossed the tightrope successfully, as did Humphrey. Near-misses only inspire other potential vice presidents to assume that their skill is greater and their luck better.

From the nation's standpoint, the political attractiveness of the vice presidency is mostly to the good. It keeps long the line of talented political leaders waiting at the door for vice presidential nominations, and that can only make the likelihood of able succession greater.

# Chapter 6
# Recommendations

The modern vice presidency is, on balance, a healthy institution. Most of its flaws are minor and can be better corrected through civic education and other informal avenues of change than through laws or constitutional amendments, although one such amendment may be desirable to clarify some harmful ambiguities in the office.

To assert a healthy vice presidency is to fly in the face of long-standing common wisdom about the office, which regards it as variously pitiful, ridiculous, or contemptible and in need of either strong legal buttressing or outright abolition. This view of the vice presidency has prompted a number of proposals for dramatic reform. Some would alter the procedures for vice presidential selection, stripping the power to nominate from the parties' national conventions and entrusting it to primaries, national committees, or even the president and Congress. Others target the activities and, sometimes, the constitutional status of the vice presidency. The reforms these critics suggest range from assigning new powers and duties to the office to redefining it as a purely executive (or purely legislative) position or even to encouraging vice presidents to assume a stance of political independence. Still other reformers propose replacing existing presidential succession procedures with a special election and, in the process, jettisoning the vice presidency altogether.

The severity of the recommendations provoked by the common wisdom about the vice presidency may be justifiable. In truth, some elements of the conventional analysis seem to be persuasive. Constitutionally, the vice presidency is devoid of serious ongoing responsibilities and is unsuited by its independence for extraconstitutional executive or legislative assignments. Yet it also is charged with providing the successor to the president in the event of a presidential vacancy. How can an office, to paraphrase Vice President John Adams, so weak in *esse* be effective in *posse*—that is, how can the vice presidency attract people who are sufficiently competent and loyal to meet the requirements of the presidency and to carry out a departed president's policies, and how can it help to prepare them to do so?

This challenge, which, for most of American history, seemed unanswerable, has been well met in recent years. Most recent vice presidents and vice presidential nominees have been well qualified—philosophically compatible with the president or presidential nominee and, as often as not, more experienced in high government office. Remarkably, the twentieth-century vice presidents who have succeeded to the presidency, as a group, have been somewhat better presidents, in the minds of historians and voters, than those who were selected in the usual way. In addition, the roles and resources of the modern vice presidency are reasonably substantial and wide-ranging. The recent history of the office has been marked by some changes in law and Constitution, notably the 1949 amendments to the National Security Act, which made the vice president a member of the National Security Council, and the Twenty-fifth Amendment, ratified in 1967, which clarified the vice presidency's status as full successor to the presidency and established both the vice president's responsibilities during presidential disabilities and a procedure for filling vice presidential vacancies. These are major changes, but the main explanation for the enhanced status of the vice presidency involves the interplay of public expectations and presidential responses. Specifically, a combination of events—Vice President Harry S. Truman's dangerously unprepared succession to the presidency during World War II; constant, global postwar tensions between the United States and the Soviet Union; and new weapons technologies that make virtually instant total war possible—have raised public concern that the vice president be competent, loyal, and prepared to succeed to the presidency literally at a moment's notice. Most candidates for president, for fear of losing votes in the election or, if elected, sustaining sharp public criticism, have responded to these concerns by choosing qualified running mates and putting them to work in the administration. Those who have not done so have suffered politically.

The conditions that produced the modern vice presidency are not likely to be undone. Recent improvements in the office, although not codified in the statute books, are solidly grounded in political realities. Equally important, the conditions that have made for a generally successful vice presidency are interrelated—they constitute a fabric that could be unraveled if certain threads, however offending they may seem, were to be pulled. Thus, in 1980, the danger of entrusting the vice president with wide-ranging operational responsibilities (a possibility discussed at the Republican convention) was not that Gerald R. Ford would perform these tasks poorly—far from it—but rather that the vice presidency as an institution is ill-suited to such roles and that the office eventually would be weakened by having to perform them. Similarly, recurring pressures to name a member of a previously unrepresented group to the second spot of a national party ticket, such as those exerted by women's organizations in 1984 and by blacks in 1988, while admirable in intent, could undermine the very vice presidential competence and loyalty that have made the office an attractive resource for presidents. Other proposals that may have a certain appeal on their own terms, such as a recent suggestion to make the vice president the de facto head of the National Security Council or the secretary of state or defense, also must be examined for their implications for the entire institution.[1]

Nonetheless, some problems, mainly of vice presidential selection and presidential disability, seem uniquely suited to careful institutional surgery. Most, including the more serious ones, can be dealt with in the same way earlier problems have been, through civic education to alter public expectations and presidential practice. Some would require a new law or constitutional amendment. For some, there is no universal remedy.

## Selection

The traditional problems of vice presidential selection—poor criteria, applied in haste—for the most part have been solved. Presidential nominating contests now are usually settled well in advance of the convention. In these circumstances, candidates have more than enough time to select their running mates; they do so with ample incentive to choose political leaders whom the voters will regard as competent and loyal. Nonetheless, some presidential nominating contests may still go down to the wire, distracting the candidates from anything but the challenge at hand and making the choice of the vice presidential nominee an afterthought. Even candidates who lock up their nominations reasonably early may experience heavy pressure to select a representative of some faction of the party for the second spot on the ticket, rendering considerations of competence and loyalty secondary to the imperative of party unity.

To some degree, selection problems now contain their own remedy—the price of a poor vice presidential nomination is press criticism, negative advertising, and, ultimately, a loss of votes. But that is small comfort to the nation if both parties nominate weak vice presidential candidates, or if, out of intense support for one presidential nominee or opposition to the other, voters elect a ticket anyway and end up with a poorly qualified successor in the vice presidency. Thus, to reduce the likelihood of a hasty or weak vice presidential nomination, voters and journalists should be urged to question presidential candidates early and often about both the criteria they intend to apply in choosing a vice president and the process by which they will screen potential running mates in light of these criteria. Such questioning should be easy to accomplish, considering the recent proliferation of candidate debates and forums during the year preceding the conventions.

Situations in which vice presidents must be selected in unusual ways—Senate election, national party nomination, or appointment under the Twenty-fifth Amendment—arise infrequently; thus, the problems that they create may seem less in need of attention. But procedural certainty actually may be most necessary in these situations precisely because they do not occur often—citizens are bound to be confused about what is supposed to happen when a vice president or vice presidential candidate dies or resigns and should not have their bewilderment compounded by ambiguities inherent in the procedures themselves. Specifically, Congress should pass legislation, as called for by the Twentieth Amendment, Section 4, to empower the national political parties to replace any candidate for president or vice president who dies either before Congress counts the electoral votes and declares a president-elect and vice-president-elect on January 6 or, if no candidate receives a majority of electoral votes, afterward. Congress also, as part of an omnibus constitutional amendment, should consider revising the Twenty-fifth Amendment to impose a ninety-day limit for congressional confirmation of vice presidential appointments, lest the amendment's original purpose of always having a vice president available in situations of succession and disability be undermined. Under this amendment, if Congress failed to act by the end of the period, the nomination would be confirmed. The omnibus amendment also should modify the Twenty-fifth Amendment to permit no more than one appointed vice president per term, to prevent the presidency from having as successor someone who was neither elected by the people nor appointed by the president whom the people did elect.

## Disability

The issue of presidential disability is inherently vexing. To transfer a president's powers and duties to someone else, even though the transfer is temporary and to the vice president, is no small matter, psychologically or politically. To tie such a transfer to a declaration of inability compounds the difficulties. The Twenty-fifth Amendment deals with the disability issue forthrightly in Sections 3 and 4 by creating procedures both to transfer and restore presidential power and to determine the existence of a disability; these procedures probably cannot be improved.

But even the best procedures are not self-executing. During the two clear occasions of presidential disability that arose under President Reagan, the barriers to effective implementation of Sections 3 and 4 became clear. For fear of appearing weak and creating public confusion, the president and his aides refused to transfer power to Vice President George Bush after Reagan was shot; they did so only grudgingly when Reagan entered the hospital for cancer surgery four years later.

The fears of the Reagan administration threaten to become self-fulfilling. If presidents treat invocations of the Twenty-fifth Amendment's disability provisions as harmful to themselves and the nation, the provisions will come to be regarded that way, rendering the amendment useless in most circumstances. Instead, presidents should be encouraged—again, the election campaign is the time to pin them down—to invoke the amendment routinely, whenever medical procedures take them out of commission for even an hour or two. If they do so, they will educate and accustom the nation to disability, and perhaps win political credit for acting prudently. If they fail to do so, they should be strongly criticized in Congress, the press, and other public forums.

A curious omission in the Twenty-fifth Amendment is any provision for vice presidential disabilities. As noted earlier, an important purpose of the amendment was to assure that a vice president would always be available to succeed to a vacant presidency or fill in for a disabled president. Even a briefly disabled vice president would be inadequate to either task; to have a vice president who was suffering from a long-term or permanent disability would undermine the Twenty-fifth Amendment entirely.

The Twenty-fifth Amendment offers a convenient model for a solution to the problem of the disabled vice president that could be included in the proposed omnibus constitutional amendment. Very simply, either the vice president or the president and a majority of the heads of the executive departments could declare the vice president disabled. During the disability, the secretary of state (or, if the secretary did not meet the constitutional qualifications for vice president, the secretary of defense, and so on) would become acting president in a situation of presidential vacancy or disability, but would not assume the vice president's Senate responsibilities. The disability would end when the vice president declared it ended, unless the president and cabinet disagreed, in which case Congress would settle the issue, as it would in a situation of disputed presidential disability. In the unlikely event that the secretary of state was serving as acting president when the vice presidential disability ended, the vice president would resume the office's successorship duties.

## Conclusion

Reform of the vice presidency is a long-standing topic of American political discourse. Modern-day reformers confront a curious state of affairs. Most important historical problems of the vice presidency—notably, poor vice presidential selection and inadequate preparation to be president—have been allayed, if not solved. Other problems of the office probably admit of no general solution. For example, the same public advocacy role that offers vice presidents such powerful political benefits within the party and the administration risks making them appear to be servile, divisive figures, inadequate to unify and lead the nation either by succession or election. This problem can be alleviated by the political sensitivity, even artistry, of individual presidents and vice presidents, not by political reform.

Somewhere between these two extremes are the problems of the vice presidency that can be eased through purposeful action. Legislation to fulfill Section 4 of the Twentieth Amendment would solve one such problem, that of the presidential or vice presidential candidate who dies before Congress declares (or, in the event of an electoral college deadlock, decides on) a president-elect and vice-president-elect. An omnibus constitutional amendment to correct certain defects in the Twenty-fifth Amendment would solve others. Specifically, the amendment would include a provision for vice presidential disabilities, place a time limit on congressional confirmation of vice presidential appointments, and limit to one the number of appointed vice presidents per term. But it is in civic education that the greatest opportunities for continued improvement in the vice presidency lie. Citizens should be taught, so that they in turn can teach those who would lead them, that presidents and presidential candidates have no excuse either to choose vice presidents rashly or to prepare them inadequately to be president and that routine invocations of the Twenty-fifth Amendment's provisions for presidential disability are to be encouraged, not avoided.

# Notes

## Chapter 1

1. Woodrow Wilson, *Congressional Government* (Boston: Houghton Mifflin, 1901), p. 240. Originally published in 1885.

2. Clinton Rossiter, *The American Presidency*, rev. ed. (Baltimore: Johns Hopkins University Press, 1987), pp. 134-35. Originally published in 1960.

3. Joel K. Goldstein, *The Modern American Vice Presidency* (Princeton, N.J.: Princeton University Press, 1982); various annual editions of *The Gallup Poll* (Wilmington, Del.: Scholarly Resources, 1982-87).

4. Paul C. Light, *Vice-Presidential Power: Advice and Influence in the White House* (Baltimore: Johns Hopkins University Press, 1984); Joseph Pika, "A New Vice Presidency?" in Michael Nelson, ed., *The Presidency and the Political System*, 2d ed. (Washington, D. C.: Congressional Quarterly Press, 1987), pp. 462-81.

5. Arthur M. Schlesinger, Jr., *The Imperial Presidency* (New York: Popular Library, 1974), p. 479.

6. Quotations from Goldstein, *Modern American Vice Presidency*, pp. 137-38.

## Chapter 2

1 This history is drawn from numerous sources, the most noteworthy of which are: Joel K. Goldstein, *The Modern American Vice Presidency* (Princeton, N.J.: Princeton University Press, 1982); Paul C. Light, *Vice-Presidential Power: Advice and Influence in the White House* (Baltimore: Johns Hopkins University Press, 1984); Irving G. Williams, *The Rise of the Vice Presidency* (Washington, D. C.: Public Affairs Press, 1956); and Max Farrand, *The Records of the Federal Convention of 1787*, 4 vols. (New Haven: Yale University Press, 1966).

2. Delegates also found that it was easier to favor legislative selection in priniciple than in practice. To give each legislator one vote in a joint election of the House of Representatives and the Senate would favor the large states; to do otherwise would favor the small states.

3. Farrand, *Records of the Federal Convention*, vol. 2, p. 537.

4. To avoid an obvious conflict of interest, an exception was made for impeachment trials of the president, during which the chief justice of the Supreme Court presides. The reason presiding officers customarily voted only to break ties was to assure that votes would not end in ties.

5. Farrand, *Records of the Federal Convention*, vol. 2, p. 537.

6. Quoted in Goldstein, *Modern American Vice Presidency*, p. 6.

7. The Twelfth Amendment also stipulated that if none received a majority of electoral votes for vice president, then "from the two highest numbers on the list, the Senate shall choose the Vice President; a quorum for the purpose shall consist of two-thirds of the whole number of Senators, and a majority of the whole number shall be necessary to a choice." The amendment's final provision regarding the vice presidency extended the original Constitution's age, citizenship, and residency requirements for president to the vice president.

8. Quoted in Thomas E. Cronin, "Rethinking the Vice Presidency," in Cronin, ed., *Rethinking the Presidency* (Boston: Little, Brown, 1982), p. 326. Rather than being buried, of course, Webster would have succeeded to the presidency when Zachary Taylor died in 1850.

9. Quoted in Williams, *Rise of the Vice Presidency*, p. 66.

10. Robert K. Murray and Tim H. Blessing, "The Presidential Performance Study: A Progress Report," *Journal of American History* 70, no. 4 (December 1983): 535-55.

11. Theodore Roosevelt, "The Three Vice-Presidential Candidates and What They Represent," *Review of Reviews* (September 1896): 289.

12. Charles Dawes announced before his inauguration that he would not accept an invitation from Calvin Coolidge to meet with the cabinet, if one were proffered. Dawes argued that presidents should be free to consult with whomever they pleased (!) and that for him to join with the cabinet might set a precedent that would constrain future presidents. Williams, *Rise of the Vice Presidency*, pp. 134-35.

13. Franklin D. Roosevelt, "Can the Vice President Be Useful?" *Saturday Evening Post*, October 16, 1920, p. 8.

14. Williams, *Rise of the Vice Presidency*, pp. 158-59.

15. Ibid.

16. Goldstein, *Modern American Vice Presidency*, pp. 147-48.

17. *Public Papers of the Presidents* (Washington, D.C.: Government Printing Office, 1957), p. 132.

18. Joseph Pika, "A New Vice Presidency?" in Michael Nelson, ed., *The Presidency and the Political System*, 2d ed. (Washington, D.C.: Congressional Quarterly Press, 1987).

19. Rockefeller also headed the White House Domestic Council, an assignment that, like Henry Wallace's, ended in failure.

20. Paul Light calls this the "abused child syndrome." Light, *Vice-Presidential Power*, p. 108.

## Chapter 3

1. Franklin D. Roosevelt, "Can the Vice President Be Useful?" *Saturday Evening Post*, October 16, 1920, p. 8. The abolition of the two-thirds rule for presidential and vice presidential nominations helped Roosevelt to accomplish his goal, both for the reasons discussed in Chapter 2 and because it is not at all certain that he could have obtained a two-thirds vote in Wallace's favor.

2. Joel K. Goldstein, *The Modern American Vice Presidency* (Princeton, N.J.: Princeton University Press, 1982), pp. 72-75, 84-88.

3. Ibid., pp. 123-27.

4. Ibid., pp. 130-32.

5. Ibid., pp. 70-72.

6. Shortly after the 1972 Democratic convention, *Time* magazine, in its August 7 issue, captured well the nature of some vice presidential nominations:

> It is all done in a 3 a.m. atmosphere by men in shirt-sleeves drinking room service coffee—elated, frantic politicians running on sleeplessness, juggling lists, putting out phone calls, arguing in the bathrooms, trying to make their reluctant minds work wisely as they consider an afterthought: the party's nominee for Vice President for the U.S. It is the worst kind of deadline politics. . . .

7. *Official Report of the Vice-Presidential Selection Committee of the Democratic Party* (Democratic National Committee, Washington, D.C., December 19, 1973); *Report of the Study Group on Vice-Presidential Selection* (Institute of Politics, John F. Kennedy School of Government, Harvard University, Cambridge, Mass., June 14, 1976); American Bar Association Special Comitee on Electoral Reform, "Symposium on the Vice Presidency," *Fordham Law Review* 45, special issue (February 1977): 703-804.

8. Endicott Peabody, "For a Grass-Roots Vice Presidency," *New York Times*, January 25, 1974; Stuart Eizenstadt, "Alternative Possibilities of Vice Presidential Selection" (paper prepared for the Vice-Presidential Selection Committee, Democratic National Committee, Washington, D.C., October 5, 1973).

9. Statement by Sen. Mike Gavel to the Vice-Presidential Selection Committee, Democratic National Committee, September 28, 1973; Eizenstadt, "Alternative Possibilities."

10. Introduced in the Senate in 1973 by Robert Griffin as S.J. Res. 166. See his remarks in *Congressional Record* 119 (1973), p. S34795. Tom Wicker also endorsed the idea in "Two for the 25th," *New York Times*, December 20, 1974.

11. See the discussion in Goldstein, *Modern Vice Presidency*, chapter 10.

12. Allan P. Sindler, "Presidential Selection and Succession in Special Situations," in Alexander Heard and Michael Nelson, eds., *Presidential Selection* (Durham, N.C.: Duke University Press, 1987), pp. 349-50. President Ford also has urged that a time limit be placed on congressional confirmation. "Transcript of President's News Conference on Domestic and Foreign Affairs," *New York Times*, October 30, 1974.

13. Goldstein, *Modern Vice Presidency*, pp. 241-48.

14. Rep. Charles Mathias, quoted in Arthur M. Schlesinger, Jr., *The Imperial Presidency* (New York: Popular Library, 1974), p. 491.

15. Not until then does Congress count the votes and declare the winners, after an opportunity is allowed to consider objections to any of the votes. Walter Berns, ed., *After the People Vote: Steps in Choosing the President* (Washington, D.C.: American Enterprise Institute, 1983), pp. 19-20.

## Chapter 4

1. Quoted in Joseph E. Persico, *The Imperial Rockefeller* (New York: Simon and Schuster, 1982), p. 262. Such stereotypes of the vice presidency persist. In 1987, when the president's press secretary told reporters that Vice President George Bush was planning a diplomatic mission to Europe, they responded:

"Did somebody die?"

"They will die!"

"After he gets there."

"He'll have his black suit with him?"

"Is he going to [Rudolph] Hess's funeral?" *The New York Times*, September 6, 1987.

2. Paul C. Light, *Vice-Presidential Power: Advice and Influence in the White House* (Baltimore: Johns Hopkins University Press, 1984), pp. 43-44; Joel K. Goldstein, *The Modern American Vice Presidency* (Princeton, N.J.: Princeton University Press, 1982), p. 180.

3. Rowland Evans and Robert Novak, *Lyndon B. Johnson: The Exercise of Power* (New York: New American Library, 1966), pp. 305-7.

4. Dwight D. Eisenhower, *Waging Peace* (Garden City, N.Y.: Doubleday, 1965), p. 6; Richard M. Nixon, *Six Crises* (Garden City, N.Y.: Doubleday, 1962), pp. 185-86; and "Nixon's Own Story of 7 Years in the Vice Presidency," *U.S. News and World Report*, May 16, 1960, p. 98.

5. Indeed, the president has less constitutional sanction over the vice president than does Congress, which can impeach on grounds of "Treason, Bribery, or other High Crimes and Misdemeanors."

6. Quoted in Goldstein, *Modern American Vice Presidency*, p. 157.

7. Quoted in Light, *Vice-Presidential Power*, p. 33.

8. Clinton L. Rossiter, "The Reform of the Vice-Presidency," *Political Science Quarterly* 63, no. 3 (September 1948): 383-403. Cf. Rossiter, *The American Presidency*, rev. ed. (Baltimore: Johns Hopkins University Press, 1987), p. 140.

9. Quoted in Thomas E. Cronin, "Rethinking the Vice Presidency," in Cronin, ed., *Rethinking the Presidency* (Boston: Little, Brown, 1982), p. 339; Dom Bonafede, "Making the Office Significant," *National Journal*, March 11, 1978, p. 380.

10. See, for example, Joseph E. Kallenbach, *The American Chief Executive* (New York: Harper & Row, 1966), pp. 234-35.

11. Vice President Thomas R. Marshall made strong declarations on all sides of the issue: he agreed to preside over the cabinet during President Woodrow Wilson's postwar trip to Europe only after stating that he was "a member of the legislative branch" and would do so "informally and personally"; he then said on another occasion that the president "was my commander-in-chief, and his orders would be obeyed." Irving G. Williams, *The Rise of the Vice Presidency* (Washington, D.C.: Public Affairs Press, 1956), pp. 107, 110.

12. Milton Eisenhower, realizing that the president cannot assign ongoing executive responsibilities to a vice president who cannot be removed, proposed the creation of two appointed vice presidents, one for domestic policy and one for foreign policy. Such officials, of course, still would not be immune from bureaucratic infighting by the White House staff and cabinet. More seriously, recent improvements in presidential succession would be jeopardized. The constitutional vice presidency, which, under Eisenhower's proposal, would continue to exist in its current form but in much-diminished status, would be considerably less appealing to competent political leaders. Milton S. Eisenhower, *The President Is Calling* (Garden City, N.Y.: Doubleday, 1974), pp. 540-41.

13. This suggestion of Carl Kaysen is described in Arthur M. Schlesinger, Jr., *The Imperial Presidency* (New York: Popular Library, 1974), p. 476.

14. Max Farrand, *The Records of the Federal Convention of 1787* (New Haven: Yale University Press, 1966), vol. 2, pp. 536-37.

15. Quoted in Light, *Vice-Presidential Power*, p. 108.

16. Hubert H. Humphrey, "Changes in the Vice Presidency," *Current History* 67, no. 396 (August 1974): 59.

17. Light, *Vice-Presidential Power*, pp. 108-13.

18. Rossiter, *The American Presidency*, chapter 1.

19. Quoted in Light, *Vice-Presidential Power*, p. 135.

20. Ibid., pp. 201-2.

21. Historically, not all vice presidents have sought influence. But in the modern era, the only two who have not—Vice Presidents Barkley and Ford—are exceptions that demonstrate the rule. President Truman tried to involve Barkley in a variety of important administration activities, but the elderly vice president simply preferred the ceremonial duties of the office. Ford, of course, came into office at the height of the Watergate investigation and had every reason to keep his distance from the president, Richard Nixon, whom he seemed likely to succeed.

22. Joseph Pika, "A New Vice Presidency?" in Michael Nelson, ed., *The Presidency and the Political System*, 2d ed. (Washington, D.C.: Congressional Quarterly Press, 1987).

23. Quoted in Cronin, "Rethinking the Vice Presidency," p. 339.

## Chapter 5
1. The vice president also would serve as acting president in the event of a failure to elect a president, a situation that is discussed briefly in Chapter 3.

2. Joel K. Goldstein, *The Modern American Vice Presidency* (Princeton, N.J.: Princeton University Press, 1982), pp. 207-8.

3. See, for example, Ruth C. Silva, *Presidential Succession* (Ann Arbor: University of Michigan Press, 1951); Edward S. Corwin, *The President: Office and Powers*, 4th ed. (New York: New York University Press, 1957), chapter 2; and John D. Feerick, *From Failing Hands: The Story of Presidential Succession* (New York: Fordham University Press, 1965), chapter 1.

4. Max Farrand, *The Records of the Federal Convention of 1787*, vol. 2 (New Haven: Yale University Press, 1966), pp. 495, 532, 535.

5. Leonard Dinnerstein, "The Accession of John Tyler to the Presidency," *The Virginia Magazine of History and Biography* 70, no. 4 (October 1962): 447-58; Stephen W. Stathis, "John Tyler's Presidential Succession: A Reappraisal," *Prologue* 8, no. 4 (Winter 1976): 223-36.

6. Arthur M. Schlesinger, Jr., *The Imperial Presidency* (New York: Popular Library, 1974), p. 487.

7. O'Hara is quoted in Goldstein, *Modern American Vice Presidency*, p. 292; Eric F. Goldman, *The Tragedy of Lyndon Johnson* (New York: Alfred A. Knopf, 1967), p. 264.

8. Presidents Truman and Eisenhower endorsed a similar arrangement in the event of a double vacancy. Quoted in Schlesinger, *Imperial Presidency*, pp. 488-89, 497-98.

9. Ibid., pp. 471-99. Schlesinger also has made the argument for abolishing the vice presidency and substituting a special presidential election for vice presidential succession in "Is the Vice President Necessary?" *Atlantic Monthly*, May 1974, pp. 37-44; "On the Presidential Succession," *Political Science Quarterly* 89, no. 3 (Fall 1974): 475-505; and *The Cycles of American History* (Boston: Houghton-Mifflin, 1987), chapter 11.

10. Paul B. Sheatsley and Jacob J. Feldman, "The Assassination of President Kennedy: Public Reactions," *Public Opinion Quarterly* 28, no. 2 (Summer 1964): 189-215.

11. See the data reported in Erwin C. Hargrove and Michael Nelson, *Presidents, Politics, and Policy* (Baltimore: Johns Hopkins University Press, 1984), pp. 21-22.

12. Calculated from the results of the Murray-Blessing poll. Robert K. Murray and Tim H. Blessing, "The Presidential Performance Study: A Progress Report," *Journal of American History* 70, no. 4 (December 1983). Reagan was not included in the survey.

13. Allan P. Sindler, "Presidential Selection and Succession in Special Situations," in Alexander Heard and Michael Nelson, eds., *Presidential Selection* (Durham, N.C.: Duke University Press, 1987), pp. 361-62.

14. Farrand, *Records of the Federal Convention*, vol. 2, p. 427.

15. John D. Feerick, *The Twenty-Fifth Amendment* (New York: Fordham University Press, 1976), p. 9; Irving G. Williams, *The Rise of the Vice Presidency* (Washington, D.C.: Public Affairs Press, 1956), pp. 112, 114.

16. Quoted in Richard M. Nixon, *Six Crises* (Garden City, N.Y.: Doubleday, 1962), p. 168.

17. Feerick, *Twenty-Fifth Amendment*, pp. 200-202.

18. Quoted in Louis W. Koenig, *The Chief Executive*, 5th ed. (New York: Harcourt Brace Jovanovich, 1986), p. 83.

19. Lawrence I. Barrett, *Gambling with History: Ronald Reagan in the White House* (Garden City, N.Y.: Doubleday, 1983), chapter 7.

20. Quoted in Goldstein, *Modern American Vice Presidency*, p. 298.

21. Ibid., p. 11.

22. See Chapter 1, note 3.

23. As Vice President Ford remarked in 1974, "I am now surrounded by a clutch of Secret Service agents, reporters and cameramen, and assorted well-wishers. When I travel I am greeted by bands playing 'Hail Columbia' and introduced to audiences with great solemnity instead of just as 'my good friend Jerry Ford.'" Quoted in Paul C. Light, *Vice-Presidential Power: Advice and Influence in the White House* (Baltimore: Johns Hopkins University Press, 1984), p. 10.

24. Quoted in Thomas E. Cronin, "Rethinking the Vice Presidency," in Cronin, ed., *Rethinking the Presidency* (Boston: Little, Brown, 1982), p. 338.

25. Dwight D. Eisenhower, *Waging Peace* (Garden City, N.Y.: Doubleday, 1965), p. 596.

## Chapter 6

1. Kevin V. Mulcahy, "Presidents and the Administration of Foreign Policy: The New Role for the Vice President," *Presidential Studies Quarterly* 17, no. 1 (Winter 1987): 119-31. Suggestions to make the vice president head of a department were widely voiced in connection with Georgia Senator Sam Nunn's possible vice presidential candidacy in 1988.

# Index

Ability of vice presidents, 7-8, 17, 61, 72, 90; to be president, 6, 44, 68, 77, 96, 98, 101

Abolition of vice presidential office: proposal to, 4, 5-7, 83-84

Accountability, 17

Activities: of vice presidents, 4, 10-13, 22-23, 24, 33, 35-37, 62, 92, 93, 94

Adams, John, 22, 25, 26-27, 32, 62, 96

Advisory role, 4, 12, 37

Advocacy role, 36, 76, 77, 78, 83, 93

Agnew, Spiro T., 38, 45, 91; resignation of, 35, 54; as vice president, 11, 36, 46, 63, 66

*American Presidency, The* (Rossiter), 21, 73

Anderson, Clinton, 63

Appointment: of vice presidents, 36, 42, 47, 49, 50-51, 53-55, 98, 100

Arthur, Chester A., 7, 30, 31, 81

Balancing of electoral ticket. *See* Ticket balancing

Barkley, Alben W., 36, 38

Budget: and vice presidential office, 12, 36, 63, 76

Burr, Aaron, 5, 28, 29

Bush, George, 7; as acting president, 70-71, 89-90, 91, 99; as presidential candidate, 3, 9, 38, 93; as vice president, 37, 44, 68; vice presidential activities, 36, 67, 73, 75, 77-78, 106n1

Butler, Nicholas Murray, 58

Cabinet, 15, 18, 87-89, 100; relations with vice president, 28, 31, 32, 36, 107n11

Caddell, Patrick, 45

Calhoun, John C., 30, 54

Carter, Jimmy, 8, 9, 37, 44-45, 72, 74-75, 76

Civic education, 100-101

Clinton, George, 10

Colfax, Schuyler, 10

Competence. *See* Ability

Congress, 22, 52-54, 98 (*See also* House of Representatives; Senate); and confirmation hearings, 14, 50, 54-55, 60; and death of presidential candidates, 85-86, 100; and presidential disability, 87-88; relations with vice president, 15, 31, 33, 36, 53, 55, 75, 81

Constitution, 5, 10, 17, 25, 28, 31, 42, 53, 96 (*See also* specific amendments, e.g. Twentieth Amendment); Article I, 62; Article II, 18, 64, 68, 80-81, 86; revisions proposed to, 56-57; 69, 100

Constitutional Convention, 5, 6, 26-27, 31, 69, 80-81

Constitutional status: of vice presidential office, 21, 23, 34, 37-38, 48, 65, 73, 77, 95-96

Coolidge, Calvin, 7, 22, 32, 33-34, 81

Curtis, Charles, 32, 34, 43, 91

Dallas, George M., 29

Dawes, Charles, 32, 34, 43, 104n12

Death: of nominee, 57, 58, 85-86, 100; of president, 22, 31, 32, 53, 81-82, 91; of vice president, 10

Democratic party, 33, 47, 54, 58, 63

Disability: of president, 14-15, 22, 31, 38, 53, 62, 70-71, 83, 86-91, 97, 99-100; of vice president, 90, 99-100

Dole, Robert, 45, 92

Duties of vice president. *See* Activities, of vice president

Eagleton, Thomas F., 38, 47, 48

Eisenhower, Dwight D., 10, 35, 64, 66, 75, 92, 94; disability of, 53, 87

Eisenhower, Milton, 107n13

Election criteria, 41-49, 51, 52, 59, 71, 82, 97-98

Electoral college, 5, 26, 28, 42, 53, 57, 80, 82

Electoral succession, 22, 28, 32, 38, 43, 44, 77, 78, 91-94
Executive power, 10, 64. *See also* Presidential power; vice presidential power
Executive responsibilities, 4, 22-23, 24, 33, 61-62, 64-69, 74-75, 77-78

Fairbanks, Charles W., 32, 34
Ferraro, Geraldine A., 38, 46
Fillmore, Millard, 7, 31, 82
Ford, Gerald R., 9, 45, 68, 97; as president, 14, 22, 65-66, 75, 82; as presidential candidate, 3, 7, 32, 38, 46, 48; rating of, 7, 33; as vice president, 12, 35, 36, 54, 55, 66, 109n23
France, 83, 84

Garfield, James A., 30, 81, 86
Garner, John Nance, 4, 21, 22, 23, 32, 33, 34, 35, 43
Gerry, Elbridge, 30, 69
Goldman, Eric, 82-83
Goldstein, Joel, 35
Gonzalez, Henry B., 90
Governance criteria, 41-49, 51, 54, 59, 61, 72, 82. *See also* Ability of vice presidents

Haig, Alexander, 67, 89
Hamlin, Hannibal, 29
Harding, Warren G., 32, 81
Harrison, William Henry, 6, 31, 81
Hayes, Rutherford B., 29
Hayden, Carl, 53
Hendricks, Thomas A., 10
Hobart, Garret A., 29, 30
Hoover, Herbert, 34
House of Representatives, 28, 56-57, 82
Humphrey, Hubert H., 7, 47, 48; as presidential candidate, 3, 92, 93, 94; as vice president, 46, 72; vice presidential activities, 36, 37, 66, 67

Importance: of vice presidential office, 23, 62-63, 73, 92
Independence: of vice presidential office, 39, 64-69, 77-78, 93, 94, 95-96
Influence: of vice presidential office, 23, 34, 62, 65, 74, 77
Institutionalization: of executive assignments, 67-68; of vice presidential office, 6-7, 12, 22, 36-37, 70, 73-76, 93; of Senate, 63

Jackson, Andrew, 29
Jefferson, Thomas, 5, 23, 28, 10
Johnson, Andrew, 7, 30, 31, 81
Johnson, Lyndon B., 7, 63; as president, 22, 39, 53, 82; as presidential candidate, 32, 38, 92; rating of, 7, 12, 33; as vice president, 36, 37, 44, 67, 69, 71, 72
Johnson, Richard M., 30, 56
Jordan, Len, 63

Kefauver, Estes, 7, 44, 49
Kennedy, John F., 36, 53, 67, 71, 82, 87
King, William R., 10
Kirbo, Charles, 45, 64-65

Lansing, Robert, 86
Legislative responsibilities, 10, 24, 33, 62-63, 69. *See also* President of the Senate
Legitimacy criteria, 14, 41, 42, 46-47, 49, 50, 54, 58, 59, 84-85
Light, Paul, 72
Lincoln, Abraham, 29, 81
Lodge, Henry Cabot, 7, 44, 68, 92

Madison, James, 30, 80
Marshall, Thomas R., 4, 21, 23, 32, 34, 86, 107n11
McCormack, John W., 53
McGovern, George, 46, 47, 58
McKinley, William, 29, 31-32, 81, 91
Mondale, Walter, 7; as presidential candidate, 38, 45, 46, 92; as vice president, 8, 12, 23-24, 44, 68, 73, 78, 79, 92-93; vice presidential activities, 36, 37, 66, 74-75, 76, 77
Morris, Gouverneur, 69
Muskie, Edmund, 92

National Security Council (NSC), 35, 66-67, 96, 97
News media, 8, 10, 31, 43, 47, 51, 60, 66, 72, 92, 98
Nixon, Richard M., 55; as president, 35, 39, 54, 82; as presidential candidate, 3, 38, 46, 68, 91, 92, 93, 94; as vice president, 12, 22, 87; vice presidential activities, 10, 36, 64, 66, 67, 75
Nunn, Sam, 109n1

Party leaders, 10, 29, 32, 33, 42, 46
Pika, Joseph, 77, 78
Plumer, William, 29
Political ads, 8, 45
Political constraints, 6, 62, 71-73
Political conventions, 33, 42, 43-44, 47-48, 49, 50, 58, 68, 97
Political leaders, 16; nomination for vice presidency of, 30, 49, 50, 52, 71, 74, 77, 94, 97; refusal of vice presidential nomination by, 29-30, 43, 68

Political parties, 5, 27, 28, 29, 42, 55, 56, 83, 85. (*See also* Democratic party; Republican party); and vice presidential selection, 29, 32, 58-59, 68

Political party unity, 41, 42, 46, 51, 71, 97

Political stability, 84-85

Political system: position of vice president in, 4, 22, 28, 77

Polk, James K., 29

President of the Senate, 6; vice president's role as, 23, 27-28, 30, 33, 62-63, 69, 83

Presidential candidates, 7, 59, 92. *See also* Electoral succession; Vice presidential selection, by presidential candidates

Presidential power, 18, 86, 89; assumption of by vice president, 8, 22, 28, 38, 62, 70-71, 80, 87, 89, 93; resumption by president, 87, 88, 89

Presidential selection, 26, 84

Presidential succession, 18, 26-27, 35, 52-53, 107n13; vice president's role in, 5, 13-15, 22, 24, 30-31, 37-38, 62, 69-70, 79-86. *See also* Successor presidents

Presidents: relations with vice presidents, 10-13, 29, 35-37, 39, 44, 64-67, 69, 71, 74-76, 77-78, 92, 93

Problems: of vice presidential office, 23-24, 97-100

Public advocacy. *See* Advocacy role

Public opinion, 22, 39, 45, 50, 60; on vice presidential competency, 8, 9, 34, 44, 53, 61, 79

Qualifications: for president, 93; for vice president, 9, 11, 34-35, 44, 45-46, 57, 68-69, 71-72, 96, 97, 98

Randolph, Edmund, 80

Rating: of successor presidents, 7, 31, 33-34, 85, 96

Reagan, Ronald: disability of, 70, 71, 89-90, 91, 99; as president, 37, 44; as presidential candidate, 9, 45, 46, 48, 68, 72

Regan, Donald, 70

Republican party, 58, 75, 92, 97

Resignation: from office, 35, 54, 82

Responsibilities: of vice presidential office, 4, 11-13, 16, 27, 31-32, 64-67, 70, 74, 77, 92, 95, 96-97. *See also* Executive responsibilities; Legislative responsibilities

Rockefeller, Nelson A., 38, 91; as vice president, 12, 14, 35, 36, 37, 54, 55, 72; vice presidential activities, 11, 62, 63, 65-66, 75

Role of vice president, 4, 6, 10, 13, 17, 25, 32, 39, 73-76, 77, 92, 96; opinion of, 23-24, 28, 30, 32-33, 62, 68, 69, 78, 82-83

Roosevelt, Franklin D., 32-33, 34, 43-44, 64, 65, 81-82

Roosevelt, Theodore: as president, 22, 31-32, 33, 34, 81, 91; rating of, 7, 33; as vice president, 25, 31, 43

Rossiter, Clinton, 21, 68, 73-74, 77

Rumsfeld, Donald, 66

Scandals: and vice presidents, 30, 54, 56, 91

Schlesinger, Arthur M., Jr., 83

Seal of vice presidential office, 37

Senate, 27-28, 42, 56, 57, 60, 63. *See also* President of the Senate

Sherman, James S., 42, 58, 91

Sherman, Roger, 27, 32, 34

Shriver, Sargent, 48, 58, 92

Sparkman, John, 44

Speaker of the House, 52, 53

Special election for succession: proposal for, 5-6, 18, 82-85

Staff (*See also* White House staff); of vice president, 12, 22, 36, 63, 68, 73, 76

Status of vice presidential office, 4, 32, 38, 52

Stevenson, Adlai, 49

Strength of vice presidential office. *See* Weaknesses of vice presidential office, strengthening of

Successor presidents, 3, 7, 22, 31, 32, 43, 79, 81-82. *See also* Rating: of successor presidents

Taft, William Howard, 34, 42

Taggert, Samuel, 29

Taylor, Zachary, 82

Tecumseh curse, 81

Ticket balancing, 8, 29-30, 32, 34, 38, 42-43, 46, 72

Tompkins, Daniel D., 10

Transfer of power, 14-15, 70, 86, 90, 99, 100. See also Presidential power, assumption by vice president;

Twenty fifth Amendment

Truman, Harry S.: as president, 18, 22, 25, 35, 35, 44, 53, 81-82, 89, 96; as presidential candidate, 32, 38; rating of, 7, 33; as vice president, 34

Tumulty, Joseph, 86

Twelfth Amendment, 5, 6, 29, 42, 56, 57, 82

Twentieth Amendment, 34, 50, 57, 58, 82, 85, 86, 92, 100

Twenty-fifth Amendment, 4, 13-15, 22, 23, 24, 35, 36, 37-38, 42, 47, 49, 52-54, 55, 57, 58, 60, 70, 82, 87-91, 96, 98, 99, 100, 101

Twenty-second Amendment, 38, 82, 92

Tyler, John, 6, 7, 31, 81, 86

Unusual selection, 52-54, 60, 98; criticism of, 54-59

Usual selection, 42-46, 59-60, 97-98; reforms proposed for, 46-52

Vacancies: in presidential office, 5-6, 13-14, 18, 37-38, 83 (*See also* Presidential succession); in vice presidential office, 22, 23, 35, 42, 52, 54, 83

Van Buren, Martin, 3-4, 9, 29, 38, 43, 56, 91

Vice presidential power, 4, 23, 25, 30, 39, 62, 67-68, 80, 83-84

Vice presidential selection, 7-10, 28-29, 31, 32, 38, 41-42, 97, 101 (*See also* Appointment; Unusual selection; Usual selection; Vacancies); haste in, 17-18, 23, 47-48, 49-50, 51-52, 58-59, 97, 98; by presidential candidates, 3, 33, 34-35, 44-45, 51, 60, 97; renomination of incumbents, 42-43, 51

Voter participation: in vice presidential selection, 48-49, 50, 52, 56

Voters' preferences, 22, 39, 60, 85, 91-92, 93, 97, 98

Wallace, Henry A., 11, 33, 44, 65

Warren, Earl, 7

Washington, George, 28

Webster, Daniel, 29-30

Weaknesses in vice presidential office, 21, 29, 34, 62, 73, 83, 97; strengthening of, 35, 36-37, 70

Wheeler, William A., 29

White House staff, 61, 84, 90; relations with vice president, 23, 66, 70-71, 72-73, 75, 76, 78, 86, 89, 99

Williamson, Hugh, 26

Wilson, Henry, 10

Wilson, Woodrow, 21, 32, 107n11; disability of, 34, 86, 87